HOLD YOUR BREATH, CHINA

HOLD YOUR BREATH, CHINA

Qiu Xiaolong

This first world edition published 2020
in Great Britain and the USA by
SEVERN HOUSE PUBLISHERS LTD of
Eardley House, 4 Uxbridge Street, London W8 7SY.
Trade paperback edition first published
in Great Britain and the USA 2020 by
SEVERN HOUSE PUBLISHERS LTD.

British Library Cataloguing in Publication Data
A CIP catalogue record for this title is available from the British Library.

ISBN-13: 978-0-7278-9043-6 (cased)
ISBN-13: 978-1-78029-691-3 (trade paper)
ISBN-13: 978-1-4483-0416-5 (e-book)

Typeset by Palimpsest Book Production Ltd.,
Falkirk, Stirlingshire, Scotland.

For my friends Yesi and Lingjun, two victims of China's air pollution.

DAY ONE
MONDAY

Detective Yu Guangming of the Shanghai Police Bureau was dragging his feet toward the bureau meeting room early Monday morning.

As the police officer in practical charge of the Special Case squad, he was far from eager to attend the first joint meeting of his team and the Homicide squad. In fact, Yu was both upset and worried, his mood almost as foul as the smoggy air outside.

It was upsetting that a serial murder case, initially reported to the Special Case squad three weeks ago, had been assigned instead to the Homicide squad under Detective Qin Xiejun.

What had happened since was no less upsetting. Qin and his people had proved not to be up to the job, having wasted three weeks with no progress made at all, and with two more bodies found in a similar manner in the early mornings.

As a result, Party Secretary Li Guohua, the number one Party boss of the bureau, wanted Detective Yu, as well as his long-time partner and personal friend, Chief Inspector Chen Cao, to help. They were supposed to serve as something like informal consultants, but with the case still under the charge of Qin's squad, and with the implication that the credit went to Qin's squad if and when the case came to be solved.

For Yu, however, that was not his main concern. He was more worried for Chen.

It was another ominous sign for the chief inspector. Once a rising star in the system, Chen was now being seen as having fallen out of the Party's grace. It was because of several successful anti-corruption investigations, ironically, involving high-ranking Party officials. With the conclusions not being what the high-above had wanted to see, Chen was noted down in an inside 'blacklist' as one who stubbornly pushed the investigations to the end – in his own way – in the name of law and justice, but not in the interests of the Party.

All of a sudden, consequently, Chen was shelved, though nominally still a chief inspector. He was quite well known as a capable, honest cop in the city. It could possibly backfire if he was too quickly removed from the position, but it made a different story to start by barring him from any politically sensitive investigations.

At least no one outside the circle would have known anything about it. Party Secretary Li was too shrewd a Party boss.

Yu thought he could guess the reason behind the arrangement made by Li. For the present case, presumably a serial murder, Chen was a most qualified investigator, having done similar investigations before, but this being a case with potential political complications presented Chen as an unreliable choice in the eyes of Li. However, the lack of any progress in the investigation, bodies piling up, the speculations about it abuzz on the Internet, all put increasing pressure on Li, who had to turn to Chen for help.

Chen must have known about the bureau politics only too well, but the inspector appeared nonchalant in the meeting room, sipping at his tea against an erratic light streaming in through the blinds. He had text-messaged Yu to request his participation in the case discussion with Qin, who was waiting there with files spread out on the long desk.

Qin nodded with a slight frown upon Yu's entrance, choosing not to say anything immediately.

After two or three minutes, Li also stepped in. Nodding at the chief inspector, the Party secretary took the seat beside him and turned to Qin opposite,

'Please go over the basic facts for our chief inspector, and for all of us, Detective Qin.'

Qin started with an involuntary cough, an effort to clear more than his throat.

'As you may have known, the first victim appeared about three weeks ago. She's a night caregiver at the Number One People's Hospital. Peng Nian, that's her name. Her body was discovered east of Bund Bridge before six in the morning. Close enough, with quite a number of people and vehicles moving around in the early hours. It's not a likely place for murder. Similar with the time – in the morning. As for the cause of death, a single blow from behind with something like a heavy brick. Her skull was fractured. Several minutes later, about five forty-five, a passerby noticed and reported her lying there unconscious, but when the ambulance arrived there was no sign of life in her.'

'A night caregiver – you mean Peng took care of patients in the hospital, but not as a nurse?' Li cut in with something not exactly like a question.

'Yes, some patients need looking after twenty-four hours. It's too much for the nurses there, and for the patients' families too. A tough job, but Peng had no choice, what with her husband paralyzed in bed, and with her son being a twenty-three-year-old dependent addicted to computer games. That morning, after having finished the night shift at the hospital, Peng was walking back home—'

'How can you have ruled out the possibility of some street mugging?' Li questioned again, apparently anxious to assert his number one position in the bureau, though with little knowledge about *real* police investigations.

'Well, she was far from a well-to-do one. Nor dressed like one. If anything, she looked more like a poor rustic "country auntie". She had to do all the dirty work for the patients there, as you can imagine.' Qin put a picture on the table. 'So we could pretty much rule out the possibility of any chance mugging for money.'

So far it had been going on like an exclusive discussion between Qin and Li. Yu looked at Chen, who seemed to be quite content with the role of patient listener, wearing an unfathomable look on his face.

'She lived in that area?' Li asked again.

'No, in the Minghang area. She had to take the bus, and then the subway to Minghang, but to save a few pennies she chose to walk to the subway station on Nanjing Road, I think.' Qin went on after a short pause, 'And there may be another possibility for that. She did hourly jobs for several families as cleaner, cooker or nanny during the day. So she could have been on the way to one of the families.'

'What else did you find?'

'Initially, we did not take it as a serial murder case, though we did notice something unusual about the timing and the location, as I've mentioned. Then the second victim turned up about a week later. A weather anchorman named Linghu at the weather bureau, in the city government building.'

'In the city government building at the People's Square,' Li echoed mechanically. 'What do you think, Chief Inspector Chen?'

'Me? I've hardly learned anything about the case – not until this morning,' Chen said. 'Please move on, Detective Qin.'

'Go on, Detective Qin,' Li said, nodding.

'We were talking about Linghu. According to one of his colleagues, Linghu had stayed overnight in the office, studying the formation of a sandstorm from the north with its potential impact on Shanghai. But according to another, Linghu stayed there for an international phone call to his friend in the States. It's free in the office.

'Whatever the reason, Linghu left the building at five thirty that morning, as recorded by the surveillance camera there. Around five forty, his body was found at the west end of the square, close to the subway station entrance. It's walking distance – four or five minutes – from the office building.'

'An even more central location, with several entrances to the subway station,' Li commented again for emphasis.

'Yes, the criminal has to be one capable of striking out with lightning speed. Like before, a single fatal blow, and the murderer disappeared into thin air—'

'Not that thin air, I'm afraid; quite murky with the morning smog of late,' Yu could not help cutting in for the first time. 'That's one of the reasons, I guess, why it was not witnessed by others.'

'But it's not that smoggy every morning,' Qin grumbled. 'We've checked the weather record.'

'Whatever air quality, what made the two connected?' Li said, putting down the tea mug on the desk with a thump.

'No connection. For the social status, no comparison imaginable between an anchorman and a night caregiver. But each of the crimes was committed in the early morning, and at a central location of the city. Similar in the cause of death, too. Some heavy object hit against the back of the head, but the wound size appeared to be much smaller for the second victim, more like from a hammer.'

'What about the possibility of copycat?' Li commented again, possibly more out of the need to say something as the Party boss.

Yu could not shake the feeling that the Party secretary could have discussed – or rehearsed – all that with Qin.

Then why such a show in the meeting room? Perhaps Li was worried that Chen would not be willing to cooperate after the case had been taken away from the Special Squad. No one would have been pleased with the bureau politics, but Yu did not think Chen would refuse to help when a serial murderer remained at large.

'What about the third victim?' Li raised the question again.

'She's a girl named Yan, in her mid-twenties, working as a sales manager of a real estate agency. Again, murder in the early morning. Before six. Near Lujiazui. One single blow, possibly from the same hammer.'

'Another victim going back home from a night shift?'

'No, she was jogging.'

'Jogging in the horrible morning air like this?' Yu asked.

'The air in Pudong is said to be slightly better. Not too many joggers, to be sure, but she was one of them. She usually jogged early in the morning before going to the office in Zabei at eight thirty. Again, we cannot find any connection among the three of them.'

'For a young, athletic girl,' Chen commented for the first time, 'it's not that easy for the murderer to pounce on her without getting noticed. Did she put up any struggle?'

'No. We've thought about that too, but he could have pretended to be another jogger, for instance, and overtaken her at a moment with no people in sight. Anyway, with three murders in three weeks . . .'

It was then that Dong Jieyuan, Qin's assistant, sneaked into the room with hurried steps. He greeted Li and Chen before moving to whisper to Qin.

'Internal Security has just called. It's more than a serial

murder case. They confirmed it. The old vice mayor was rushed into the hospital.'

In spite of Dong's abated voice, Inspector Chen thought he overheard the words 'Internal Security', and for the last sentence, while not catching every word from Dong, something like the 'old vice mayor', which could be politically alarming.

That it was something more than a serial murder Chen had suspected at the beginning of the meeting.

'Three weeks after Peng's body was found,' Chen said deliberately. 'Three victims so far – or four?'

'Yes, we've just learned about the fourth victim,' Qin responded in a hurry. 'For reasons beyond us, Internal Security took over the case – I mean the fourth victim – three days ago without discussing it with us.'

'That was Friday.'

'Yes, we heard from Internal Security that it's a political case on Friday morning. So we did not see it as something related—'

'So it was never reported to the bureau?'

'It was, but they had already started looking into it. The victim was said to be a journalist with some sensitive information in her possession.'

'You did not discuss it with them?'

'Considering some similarities among the cases, I sent them the file about the first three murders.'

'The file we have never had any access to,' Yu cut in sarcastically.

Chen was about to say something when his cellphone started ringing in the meeting room. He took it out, looked at the number, and said apologetically to the others sitting at the long desk, 'Sorry, it's from Comrade Secretary Zhao in Beijing. I have to take it.'

Instead of rising to move out of the meeting room, Chen flipped open the phone there and then.

Party Secretary Li was watching intensely, frowning in spite of himself.

'Oh Comrade Secretary Zhao,' Chen started talking without trying to cover the phone. 'You're in Shanghai?'

'Comrade Secretary Zhao, the retired first secretary of the Party Central Discipline Committee,' Li echoed in a low voice, in response to the questioning looks from the others in the meeting room.

'You mean at this moment?' Chen went on with genuine surprise in his voice. 'But I'm in the middle of a case discussion in the bureau—'

For the next couple of minutes, Chen listened attentively, without making a comment to Zhao at the other end of the line.

'Fine, I'll come over right now. The Hyatt Hotel in Pudong. I know where it is.'

Closing the phone, Chen turned to Li.

'Comrade Secretary Zhao wants me to go over to the Hyatt Hotel in Pudong.'

'Did he mention anything specific?'

'Not on the phone. He just wants "a chitchat" with me, that's what he said, and he insisted on my going there immediately. He's just checked into the hotel this morning.'

'To chitchat with our legendary chief inspector upon his arrival in Shanghai!' Qin exclaimed.

'Comrade Secretary Zhao has such a high opinion of Comrade Chief Inspector Chen,' Li said, nodding at Chen again. 'You have no choice but to go, even though Qin is telling us about a new victim. After all, Comrade Secretary Zhao has come all the way for you from Beijing.'

Chen detected a note of frustration in Li's voice. The involvement of Internal Security seemed to shed some light on Li's urgency for the meeting this morning.

And there might be another reason for it, Chen thought. As the opening session of National People's Congress was drawing nearer, it would be a political disaster for the bureau if the case – more and more likely a serial murder case – remained unsolved, with more and more bodies piling up all the time.

'You stay on here, Detective Yu, and fill me in with the rest of the discussion. I should be back in a couple of hours,' Chen said, before turning to Qin. 'Sorry, Detective Qin, but we'll talk more about it.'

*   *   *

Inspector Chen had a hard time squeezing into the subway train to Pudong.

It was past the rush hour, but the train was still so packed – just like his mind, with possible scenarios jostling against each other.

Like the others in the bureau meeting room, Chen had no idea about Zhao's real reason for summoning him to the hotel for 'a chitchat' on the first day of his vacation in the city of Shanghai.

To Chen, Zhao had been something of a political patron, having entrusted him with several high-profile cases and backed him up on a number of occasions. Chen could have long been crushed by his adversaries, as whispered in the inner circle, but for Zhao's speaking out for him at the top.

Of late, Zhao had not been pleased with his work. Chen's insistence on judicial independence in a murder investigation against a Red Prince, disregarding the instruction from above, ruffled enough high feathers. While the successful conclusion of the investigation was hailed online as another coup of the 'brilliant inspector', Zhao had called him in the middle of the night, saying, 'It speaks volumes about your political immaturity for seeing only the tree instead of the forest.'

For today's talk with Zhao, Chen thought he had to pick and choose each and every word with utmost caution.

An unexpected lurch of the subway train nearly made a young girl standing beside him fall against him, her high heel stamping on his foot. She was listening to the music from her smartphone through the earplugs, her eyes half-closed above a large mask, and her hips swaying to the rhythm, unaware of anything else happening around her.

Still, the subway made a reliable alternative for him, though Chen had got lost on several occasions in the maze of criss-crossing lines. In a city constantly suffering traffic congestion, cars could literally crawl along the road, and he could not afford to be late for Zhao.

In less than half an hour, he found himself moving out of Lujiazui Station.

Looking up to the street sign, he thought of the body of the third victim, a young girl named Yan discovered in the area, perhaps close to the station. It was a surreal, ominous coincidence.

He was trying to shake off the premonition under the surrounding high-rises, coughing with a hand covering his mouth, when his phone started to ring.

It was Detective Yu.

'Is it OK to talk to you now?'

'It's OK. I'm just walking out of the subway station. The meeting finished?'

'The meeting was stopped because of you. After you left, they saw no point discussing too much with me.'

'You don't have to say that, Yu. You're the one in practical charge of our squad, they all know that. They were simply upset with my leaving in the middle of the meeting. Did Qin tell you something more about the fourth victim?'

'Not that much. But he did give me the file about the first three victims. It may be true that he himself has learned little about the fourth from Internal Security.'

'But why Internal Security? There are too many journalists in the city for them. Has she written anything that politically sensitive?'

'No, Qin did not say anything about that. But he said he had heard something about her husband, who's the current head of Wenxin Group, or something like that, having recently retired from the position of first vice mayor – he's more than thirty years older than Xiang. That's her name, by the way.'

'Vice Mayor Geng? So it was him that got rushed into the hospital. Internal Security must have seen that as an attack against a senior Party cadre. A political case indeed.'

'But the file sent by Qin alerted them to the possibility of her being just another victim in the serial murder case. So they compared notes. The closer examination of her head wound indicates that the blow could have been afflicted with the same weapon – a hammer.'

'That's why our Party secretary called for the meeting this morning.'

'There might have been something more. More in the murky background. Qin hemmed and hawed. At least that's the impression I got.'

'They have come to us under the pressure,' Chen said. 'Now I'm moving into the hotel. Zhao is waiting upstairs. I'll call you later.'

Inspector Chen found himself sitting, literally on pins and needles, by the window of the grand river-view suite on the thirty-ninth floor of the Hyatt Hotel in Pudong, in the company of Comrade Secretary Zhao, the retired yet still powerful first secretary of the Party Central Discipline Committee from the Forbidden City.

The bird's-eye view outside the hotel window should have been a breathtaking one, with colorful vessels sailing along the Huangpu River outlined by majestic high-rises on both sides, but for the moment there was hardly any view to speak about.

All around, the hotel seemed to be mantled with an immense pale shroud instead.

'Like everywhere else, Shanghai has changed such a lot in China's unprecedented economic reform,' Zhao said, with a suggestion of pleasant nostalgia. 'East of the river, it used to be nothing but farmland around here, I still remember so clearly. Now, with all these skyscrapers jostling against one another, it is truly the financial center of Asia, and soon, I believe, of the whole world too.'

For a man of his powerful position in the Party system, Zhao did not speak exactly in an official manner – at least not in front of Chen, who listened attentively, sitting stiffly, nodding respectfully, trying to focus on the talk, though his mind kept wandering back to the case he had been discussing in the bureau.

It was admittedly a true statement, that prelude delivered by Zhao. The dramatic transformation of the city landscape in recent years seemed so unbelievable, even to a native Shanghainese like Chen. Particularly for the area of Pudong east of the Huangpu River.

Next to the Hyatt Hotel, another new building in construction – the Shanghai Trade Center, that would reportedly be even higher than all the others, with its construction to be completed in the near future – appeared to be rising up like the genie out of the bottle. Mysterious masked workers could be seen welding high up here and there, perching precariously on the cloud-wrapped steel scaffolding, shooting out bright sparks into the grayness around them.

'Yes, people nowadays call Shanghai a "magic city" on the Internet.' Chen did not go on to say that the netizens did not use the term 'magic' always in the positive sense. There's no point discussing anything without 'positive energy' to the senior Party leader, though Zhao was sometimes described as a relatively moderate one in the Forbidden City.

'Guess why I have come to Shanghai this time?' Zhao went on, as if in response to Chen's unasked question about the unannounced visit. '"It's an old comrade's research tour", as reported in the newspapers. But between you and me, I've just had enough of the Beijing "smog" air, as it is called on the Internet – a new word in the Chinese vocabulary.'

'Well it's certainly not fog, which comes up just in the morning. Smog won't disperse, and it remains indissoluble all day long. And so unhealthy too, full of tiny toxic particles.'

'Whatever the name, the air quality is bad in the capital. I have to wear a mask going outside. So it's a much-needed change for an old man like me, a short vacation for fresh air in the south. I think I'll stay here for a week or so, and then go to Suzhou and Hangzhou.'

'But here . . .' Chen did not finish the sentence saying that *the air quality is pretty bad too.*

Compared with things in Beijing, it might not be that unbearable in Shanghai. For several days in a row, a considerable number of flights had been canceled or delayed, Chen had read, because of the extreme poor visibility caused by impenetrable smog surrounding the Beijing airport.

'Yes, that's a very good idea, Comrade Secretary Zhao. A lot of people are talking about "fresh air vacations" or "smog vacations", traveling to seaside cities for a whiff of freshening air, or to other countries for a short "lung cleansing period—"'

A low purring sound came from somewhere in the grand suite, abruptly, like a contented sigh produced by a whimsical cat after a satisfactory nap, rubbing its back against the windowpane. Chen looked around in surprise. For such a high-end hotel, the air conditioning should not have made any noise.

'Don't worry about it, Chen. It's the latest imported fresh air machine system the hotel management has installed prior to my arrival here,' Zhao said, with a subtle touch of self-satire. 'Supposedly more effective than the ordinary air purifier. It's capable of circulating the filtered naturally fresh air back into the hotel room.'

How the 'filtered' and the 'naturally fresh' could possibly co-exist in one single breath was way beyond him, but Chen knew better than to raise the question. After all, senior Party leaders like Zhao were supposed to enjoy those privileges unimaginable to ordinary people.

Whether discussing this was truly the reason behind such a 'chitchat' during Zhao's vacation to Shanghai, however, Chen still hadn't the slightest idea.

He had heard of a fierce new struggle unfolding at the pinnacle of power inside the Forbidden City, with Zhao's name mentioned in the background. At such a critical juncture, it did not make sense for someone like Zhao to take a 'fresh air vacation' out of Beijing.

Nor was it so likely that upon arrival in Shanghai, Zhao would have chosen to summon Chen over to the hotel for a chitchat.

'Unfortunately, the air quality here in Shanghai is not that good either, I know,' Zhao went on, sipping at his tea reflectively. 'I've recently read an Internet joke about a starved bird falling from the sky to the rice paddy in Qingpu County, Shanghai, because there's no food visible at all through the darkly murky air.'

'It is a problem.' Chen felt compelled to say something earnest in response. 'For several days, school children here are not supposed to go to school, or to step out in the open. The air pollution warning applies particularly to the sick or old people, as announced in the *Wenhui Daily*.'

'Yes, the problem is serious,' Zhao said, sort of echoing. 'In Beijing, the AQI index is read as unhealthy for more than six months in a year, and occasionally, even more dangerous. Far more smoggy and smoky than here, unsuitable for any activities in the open. It's quite understandable that people are complaining about it, and about the corruption too, but . . .'

There was always a 'but' in Zhao's talk; Chen knew that only too well. Zhao paused, taking a leisured sip at a cup of tea again – *Before-the-Rain* tea – before continuing, and lighting a Panda cigarette for himself. For once, Zhao did not offer one to Chen.

'But the situation should not be politicized. The current problem is a result of complicated, historical factors, in spite of the strenuous anti-pollution efforts made by our Party. It takes time to tackle the problem, you know, especially for a still fast-developing country like China. Having said that, people's concerns under the smog-smothered sky are not that unjustified, which we have to acknowledge. In short, it's an issue that needs to be addressed at a higher level, a different level.'

To Chen's alarm, this was sounding less and less like a 'chitchat'. Not from someone like Zhao. Chen hastened to pull himself together, trying to think in a whirl of confusing thoughts before he responded, speaking circumspectly.

'If it's more often than not, as in accordance to an article I've read, that our people have to breathe in foul air, drink contaminated water, and eat toxic food, how can they not complain?' Chen went on, seeing no disapproval in Zhao's expression. 'Last week, I watched a "political star scholar" arguing on a TV forum for the stratagem of having "no smog in the heart as the solution to the smog in the air", but that's no solution.'

'Well, it's just like *The Thirty-Seven Stratagems*. That's no solution, I cannot agree more with you.'

Zhao was referring to a classic work titled *The Thirty-Six Stratagems*, about the art of war in ancient China, discussing each stratagem based on a real, well-known battle in the earlier history. Chen had played with the idea of translating it into English. The stratagems were supposed to be helpful not just in war.

At least they had proven to be helpful to him in a number of difficult police investigations.

But the thirty-seventh stratagem was non-existent, which could be meant only as a joke from Zhao.

'People are trying to deal with the problem,' Zhao went on, with a sudden serious edge to his voice. 'In fact, a group of activists are secretly gathering in Shanghai, I've heard, trying to do something about it. So that will be a job for you, Comrade Chief Inspector Chen. An important job, but quite a simple one to you. To find out as much as you can about what they are trying to do in secret.'

'No, I'm no environmental expert. It's a job beyond me, I'm sorry about it, Comrade Secretary Zhao.'

It came out as an instinctive no. For one thing, an 'important job' from Zhao had never been simple. What's more, Chen could not conscientiously bring himself to spy on the people who were trying to tackle air pollution – whether in secret or not.

Taking a deep breath to make a more elaborate argument about his inadequacy for this clandestine assignment, Chen ended up, to his embarrassment, breaking into a fit of uncontrollable coughing.

'Sorry, some throat problem because of the irritation of the polluted air, I believe.'

'That's the very reason you should take the job, Chief Inspector Chen. Now, the leader of the group I've just mentioned is an attractive woman named Yuan Jing, who has recently come back from a visit to the United States.'

A visit to the United States sounded even more portentous to Chen. Whatever she was doing in Shanghai could be easily interpreted as her working in the American interest. Chen had had his share of 'sensitive details' in such political cases.

To be fair to Zhao and the people like him in Beijing, the environmental crisis was not what they would have liked to see. Whatever official propagandas or interpretations, it was happening under the rule of the 'great and glorious Chinese Communist Party'. They, too, were anxious to solve the problem.

But at the same time, it was inconceivable and intolerable for any anti-pollution attempt to be made at the possible expense of economic development, which turned out to be the one and only legitimacy for the one-Party regime. As Comrade Deng Xiaoping had put it at the very beginning of China's reform,

'The development is the one and only true argument' – the unquestionable meta-narrative for China.

'When you called into the bureau, Comrade Secretary Zhao, I was in the middle of a case discussion with my colleagues. Possibly a serial murder case, something urgent for us with the opening session of the People's Congress drawing nearer. Party Secretary Li of our bureau insists on solving the case as quickly as possible – before the grand event in Beijing. Otherwise people would be talking about the case rather than anything else. Since I have done similar investigations before, Li would probably not let me get away for anything else at this moment.'

'You have done cases like that, I know, but a murder case and the People's Congress are two different matters, and you don't have to put them together. As a young emerging cadre, you should not be concerned just with these cases, Comrade Chief Inspector Chen. Remember what the Tang dynasty poet Wang Zhihuan says in the poem on the Guanque Tower?'

'*You have to climb even higher to see further . . . thousands of miles away to the horizon.*'

'Exactly. I'll talk to Li about it. He should understand that too.'

Chen was not ungrateful with the way Zhao responded, apparently ready to throw in his weight to back the inspector again. Still, Chen hesitated.

'But it is really out of my element.'

'Don't keep on saying no, Comrade Chief Inspector Chen.' Zhao produced a large manila envelope from the pile on the desk. 'Take a look at the material inside. Yuan Jing used to be based in Wuxi, but she now has an office in Shanghai, too. A well-connected activist, as well as a super VIP on the Internet for her posts about environmental issues. It's said she has millions of online followers who forward and reforward each and every post of hers. She's quite influential.'

'She's from Wuxi?' he asked mechanically, more like an echo than a question.

'For the project she has been pursuing, some of her associates are in the city of Shanghai, including several wealthy and influential Big Bucks. You know the city and its people well, don't you?'

Chen took the envelope and pulled out a folder. The moment he opened it, unexpectedly, a color picture fell to the floor.

It seemed as if – in a moment of disorientation – something like a fortune-telling bamboo slip was falling, portentously, to the flagstone-covered ground of an ancient temple in ruins.

Chen caught himself staring at a picture of Shanshan, who was smiling back at him contemplatively.

Realization hit home. His mind briefly wandered, trying to remember the last time he saw her.

Yuan Jing was the micro-blogging name for Shanshan.

So she had come to the fore for her environmental activities and writings on the Internet in the last several years, in an unbelievable transformation, of which he had not heard anything.

Or was it simply a result of his subconscious effort to keep her out of sight, out of mind?

He was at a loss for words.

To his unexpected relief, Zhao's cellphone started ringing in the hotel suite. The senior Party leader frowned at the number and started moving to the bedroom, holding the phone in one hand and gesturing for Chen to wait with the other.

It must have been an important phone call.

With the bedroom door shut after Zhao, Inspector Chen had the large living room to himself.

Looking out the window, he still failed to catch a clear view of the river. Instead, his imagination began wandering with the waves in the Huangpu River, rolling, splashing and converging, for a fleeting moment, with the waves in Tai Lake, by which he had stood with Shanshan, her hand touching his . . .

> *What cannot be cut,*
> *nor raveled,*
> *is the sadness of separation . . .*

It was an unbelievable coincidence that his first meeting with Shanshan had also originated, more clearly in retrospect, from an environmental disaster.

That long-ago afternoon, Chen happened to be sitting at a roadside eatery, an impossible and impatient gourmet, eager to enjoy the local delicious specials – 'three whites of the lake' – when Shanshan, a young, vivacious environmental engineer at a local chemical factory, came to stop him from putting the white shrimp into his mouth. She delivered an unpleasant lecture about the lake food being seriously contaminated by the toxic water.

So it had started as an annoying wet blanket to the Epicurean inspector incognito on vacation, but an idyllic episode soon unfolded between the two of them. He found himself more than drawn toward her, an attractive, intelligent young woman with an idealistic passion for the environmental cause. The subsequent conspiracy of the circumstances pushed the two, paradoxically, further into an intimate relationship, despite the polluted lake and the diabolic murders in the background.

Like a Chinese proverb, however, eight or nine times out of ten, things in this world do not work out the way we expect. An unexpected turn in a series of deadly events toward the end of his Wuxi vacation had left him stranded in a scene from *Casablanca*, watching the woman he loved throwing herself into the arms of another man.

Confucius says: time flows away non-stop, day and night, like water in the river.

But it was not a moment to indulge himself in sentimental reminiscences of the romantic moments by Tai Lake, Chen hastened to tell himself.

He turned to cast a look at the desk. Among the books and files, he was surprised to see a copy of *Shanghai Literature* in a pile on the desk, and a red-headed document about 'The Ecological Disaster of the Petroleum Industry'.

It was then he heard the bedroom door handle turning.

As Zhao emerged from the bedroom holding the phone in his hand, Inspector Chen was just picking up the literature magazine from the desk.

'Yes, you're rereading the poem, our poet inspector.'

'What?'

'"Don't Cry, Tai Lake," right? It's really a good poem about the polluted lake in Wuxi. I like it a lot.'

'Oh . . . you are carrying that issue with you, Comrade Secretary Zhao, but that's a couple of years old.'

'Yes, I'm carrying the magazine with me. The pollution has been going from bad to worse. That's why your poem really matters,' Zhao said, taking over the magazine and opening to the page with the beginning of the poem on it. 'Tell you what, several people I know in Beijing have also read the poem. An excellent piece with a high level of ecological awareness, they all agreed with me about it.'

'Thank you so much, Comrade Secretary Zhao,' he said, not knowing what else to say.

'In face of the insurmountable problem, the characters in the poem do not just give up. That's the spirit, Chief Inspector Chen. It was written during that vacation of yours at Wuxi Cadre Recreation Center, wasn't it?'

'Yes, it was so kind of you to let me have that all-inclusive vacation, which had been originally arranged for you. I truly enjoyed it. While staying by the lakeside, I also happened to see a lot with my own eyes how disastrously the lake was polluted—'

'And you happened to find your muse for the poem, I suppose.'

What was Zhao driving at? The senior Party leader was not a man in the habit of talking about the muse for poetry or anything like that. Unable to figure it out, Chen chose to make no immediate response.

'The poem shows that you have been following the environmental issues in your conscientious way,' Zhao said, looking him in the eye, 'and that's why you will do the job. It does not require an environmental expert, but a knowledgeable, sensitive and resourceful investigator. More importantly, an honest one I can trust.'

'But writing in sentimental lines is totally different from investigating in scientific terms.'

'Well, just come up with whatever you can uncover. Afterward, you may write another environmental poem, our gifted poet inspector.'

'But what "whatever", exactly, Comrade Secretary Zhao?'
'What are they doing? Who are involved and contacted and connected? From where comes the financial support and means to their project? How far are they making progress?'
'I see.'
'More material will follow. Make sure you report to me personally. For whatever expense is involved in your work, you may have it reimbursed through the Party Central Discipline Committee, about which I've given specific instruction to my assistant in Beijing. You don't have to explain anything to him. Nor to any other people, for that matter. I've told some comrades in the Shanghai city government that you shall be keeping me company – as an experienced tourist guide – during my stay here. So you don't have to worry about your routine work in the police bureau.'

So it was an assignment to which Chen was not in a position to say no any more.

And for a personal reason, too, even more than the political reasons Zhao had just given him.

Chief Inspector Chen, Chen said to himself, *would not let any harm come to Shanshan, or Yuan Jing.*

At the same time, he wanted to find out what had happened to her since their parting in Wuxi.

'Thank you so much for your trust in me, and for your thoughtful arrangement, Comrade Secretary Zhao. I'll do my level best.'

'Now, with anything you find – anything important – call me or text me at once. You have my special cellphone number, don't you?' Zhao added, as though in afterthought, 'Some of these activists can be acting out of their concerns for the problem, so there may be nothing really wrong with their motive. I've read one of her posts online – Yuan Jing's, I mean – and it's quite well written. We don't have to jump to any political conclusion.'

'I understand, Comrade Secretary Zhao, and I'll keep you posted.'

'At the same time, they can be too recklessly pushing forward with their agenda, regardless of its consequences in today's China. And there's no ruling out, needless to say, that some of the so-called activists are taking advantage of the current situation with their ulterior political motive.'

A number of possible scenarios flashed across Chen's mind. But then others were coming up, conflicting, contradicting . . .

He rose to take leave with the folder grasped tight in his hand.

As he strode into the high-speed elevator in a hurry, he nearly stumbled, the bulging folder heavier than expected.

Emerging from the hotel, Inspector Chen decided not to take a taxi from the long line waiting for customers in front.

He was going to take a short walk first. Walking, he was sometimes capable of making a concentrated effort to think.

But it took only a couple of minutes for him to realize the mistake. The polluted air outside was horrible, and more noticeable after he had been in the luxurious hotel suite installed with the advanced fresh air system.

Moving along Century Avenue, he found it hard even to breathe, as if all the surrounding high-rises were pressing down around him. It was too uncomfortable for him to think with any clarity. The fragments of Zhao's talk kept swirling, even more entangled than before.

While Zhao did not give a hint about any knowledge regarding his relationship with Shanshan in Wuxi, his insistence on Chen taking the job – in connection to the poem – was darkly suggestive.

Nor would it have been too astonishing that the inspector, having ruffled enough high feathers, had been secretly placed under the governmental radar as early as his vacation days in Wuxi, where he was in the company of Shanshan.

So it was turning out to be something like an investigation against the investigations about him. With no other cops working under him, no official resources available, he had to grope along all by himself, employing those deceptive stratagems like in that time-honored Chinese classic *The Thirty-Six Stratagems*, maneuvering in a roundabout way, and moving stealthily without being detected by others.

'To sail across the sea undetected by the eyes in the

skies.' He thought of the first stratagem in *The Thirty-Six Stratagems*. He had no idea how he could possibly achieve that.

But his opponents had been maneuvering against him, against Shanshan.

After making several wrong turns, he caught the sign pointing to the subway station at Lujiazui, where he could take Line 1 back home, but he slowed down, stopped, and turned into a side street.

He walked for a couple of blocks before spotting a small convenience store on the corner. For the time of the day, he found himself the only customer there.

'A new SIM card,' he said, handing over three one-hundred bills to a salesgirl – double the amount for the SIM card he wanted to buy.

'Just for the SIM card?' She raised the money in her hand questioningly. According to the latest city regulation, a SIM card purchaser had to show his ID for registration.

'Yes, you can keep the change.' He nodded with a smile. It's just like in a popular Chinese saying: While the government has one regulation, people have ten counter-regulations.

Smiling back, she was about to hand him the SIM card when she said, 'Why don't you have another phone? A different one, so you won't get the two phones confused.'

'Good idea.'

'Then another seven hundred yuan. You have both the phone and the SIM card.'

'One thousand yuan for the two, right?'

It was not a small sum, but he turned over the money. So he got from her a SIM card as well as a white phone, a special one for the investigation, which would not get confused with his regular phone, a black one.

Pocketing the new phone, Inspector Chen headed toward the riverbank.

Not far from the convenience store, there was a park-like area, which was usually crowded with tourists taking or posing for pictures with the Oriental Pearl Tower in the background. For the day with the PM 2.5 level high in the air, however, it looked deserted, with few people visible.

There he came to a stop. Taking another deep breath in spite of himself, he stood leaning against the embankment and looking up.

Across the river, the Bund stretched out, with those magnificent imposing neoclassical buildings sporting time-yellowed art-deco facades, enveloped in the gray air, almost unreal, eerily reminiscent of those black and white movies made in the late twenties in the last century. It represented such a surreal scene as to galvanize him into the realistic role he was supposed to play: that of a police inspector working in secret.

But there were things in Zhao's talk that both alarmed and confused him about the role. Things that gave conflicting and foreboding signals, different from those in the *People's Daily*, which usually interpreted the environmental crisis as a temporary bump in China's marching forward along the great socialist road.

For a senior Party official on a 'research tour', Zhao could have easily had the entire Shanghai Police Bureau at his disposal if he had really wanted to do something about a group of activists. No one would have murmured anything about his 'research'.

Then why choose Chen for the job, with the insistence on secrecy, and with the deliberate cover of his serving as a 'tourist guide' during Zhao's vacation in Shanghai?

There was also something ambivalent in Zhao's attitude toward Shanshan and other activists, as if he was not so anxious to crush them in a preemptive strike – at least not until the chief inspector had found out something meaningful about them.

Not informed with Zhao's real intention, Chen could probably try to play safe by making a show of checking the activists, yet providing some selective information, which Zhao might have already obtained anyway.

But could the inspector really do that?

The river water lapping against the shore, he thought hard with an unlit cigarette in his hand, but his efforts did not yield an easy answer. Instead, he was beginning to have a dull headache.

A sudden siren came piercing the somber sky over the river, like a line in the poem.

Inspector Chen started walking again, along the bank like a tourist, before he took out the white cellphone. He changed his mind, however, at the sight of a public phone booth on another side street.

Few public phone booths were left behind and in use in the fast-changing city. As he was striding over, reaching out to pull open the dust-covered door of the booth, a young girl scampered by, eyeing him curiously, if not suspiciously, while talking non-stop to a cellphone through her white mask.

Once inside, he dialed the phone number of the *Shanghai Literature* magazine editor surnamed Ouyang.

'You have some new poems for me?' Ouyang said, more like a statement than a question.

'Not right now, but I have to ask you a favor, Ouyang. Do you still have copies of the issue that contains "Don't Cry, Tai Lake"? Some people want to read the poem.'

'I'm not at all surprised, Chief Inspector Chen. You're truly a rising star in the system. Some other people asked for the issue too. From Beijing, I remember.'

'Really! Do you remember the name of the people who contacted you about it?'

'No, just someone at a high-level government office in Beijing, that's about all I remember. He must have talked to the city propaganda ministry before contacting me. The city people later called me, too. It's a great honor, according to them, that the senior Party cadres in Beijing want to read our magazine because of your poem.'

'What else did they say to you?'

'Let me think.' Ouyang started to speak reflectively. 'The Beijing office did ask me some questions, such as whether the poem was based on your personal experience or not. I said I did not know. It's impossible to say, as you know, how much of an imaginative literary work comes from the writer's personal experience. Or at all.'

'Well said, Ouyang. That's what Eliot's impersonal theory is all about. Anything else?'

'Hold on. I may be getting things confused. It happened quite a while ago. It's possible that a couple of people – actually from different offices in Beijing – called us about your poem. They both requested copies of our magazine, I think.'

'Can you double-check that for me?'

'Of course. Our office assistant Nanhua may have kept the mailing address or addressee in the office logbook.'

'That will be great.'

'You may pick up copies any time you like – as many as you like. The more people interested in our magazine, the better. By the way,' Ouyang went on after a short pause, 'Qiang is retiring after having been in charge of the foreign liaison office here for almost forty years. I saw him yesterday, and he specifically asked about you.'

'Thanks, Ouyang,' he said, thinking Ouyang's mention of Qiang a bit out of the blue. 'I've not seen Qiang for quite a long time. A nice man, he helped me a lot in the days when I first became a member of the Writers' Association.'

Chen put back the phone, frowning again. It had been a shot in the dark. What he had just learned, however, confirmed his suspicion. People had been checking out his work, and not because of their appreciation of literature.

He knew better.

What's more, he was checked by two different groups of people in Beijing. If one inquiry was made by Zhao's office, what about the other?

Inspector Chen was ready to get out of the booth, pushing open the door, when the big clock on top of the custom house across the river began striking the hour.

As if in an inexplicable correspondence with the chime, another thought struck him. So he stepped back into the booth and picked up the phone again.

This time he dialed the number of Little Huang, a young cop he had met in Wuxi during his vacation there.

Detective Huang, a passionate fan of Sherlock Holmes, and perhaps even more so of 'Master Chief Inspector Chen', had his imagination too much enriched with the mystery novels he devoured, and in his eyes, what the Shanghai inspector had done during the Tai Lake murder investigation simply put him on the same par as any fictional 'Master'.

As requested, Huang immediately called back to the number of the Shanghai public phone booth from a public phone booth in Wuxi. The young cop started with undisguised excitement in his voice,

'Another confidential case, Chief Inspector Chen?'

'Confidential, yes. It's so confidential I can hardly give you any details, except that it's directly from Beijing. That's about all I can say at the moment. But it's not exactly a case; not yet, at this moment. To start with, I want to know what has happened to Shanshan in Wuxi. You know whom I'm talking about, don't you?'

'Oh, Shanshan. Of course I know.' Huang began to sound even more excited. 'Since you left Wuxi at the end of that investigation, I have made a point of inquiring about her from time to time. Not that directly, as you may imagine. More than two years ago, or perhaps even earlier, it was said that she was going to study for a PhD degree in the UK. Sure enough, she came to the local police bureau to apply for the passport for that purpose. With her name still on the governmental blacklist, it could have been extremely difficult for her to obtain the passport, so I helped to smooth her application process without her knowledge.'

'Good job, Little Huang. I appreciate it. But she did not leave for the UK as she had planned. Right?'

'No. She did not. Shortly after she obtained the passport, she married a local businessman surnamed Yao.'

'She married—'

Chen checked himself from finishing the sentence. For an attractive, intelligent young woman like Shanshan, that was nothing to be surprised about.

'Sorry, I thought about calling you at the time, Chief Inspector Chen, but things happened to get so busy here with a political case.'

He could guess the reason why Huang had chosen not to upset him with the news. The Wuxi cop knew a thing or two about the relationship. But it was a closed chapter, at least so it seemed to the young cop, no point opening it again.

'You don't have to say sorry for that. So she's married with someone surnamed Yao?'

'Yes. Yao runs a successful solar energy company in Wuxi. Possibly the number one in the country. She stayed on with him, helping to take care of his business instead of working at that local chemical factory. She also started making frequent trips to Shanghai for her husband's business, I think. In the meantime, she has become an "Internet celebrity" or a "public intellectual" for her online writing about environmental issues, all of which I've learned from a net cop stationed in Wuxi. His name is Bei, and he occasionally goes to Shanghai too – most likely because of her. She's still being closely watched by government people, I suppose.'

'That's no surprise. But there was another man quite close to her at the time. I mean during the days I was on vacation, staying at the Wuxi Cadre Recreation Center.'

'You mean the man she saw before Yao? Yes, you actually insisted on my helping to arrange a meeting between the two the day he was sent to prison – Jiang, I think that's his name. It's just so magnanimous of you, I have to say. Hold on—' Huang paused with a light click, and then a light ding, conceivably from a smartphone in his hand inside the public phone booth, checking something quickly.

'Yes, Jiang was an environmental activist. He brought big trouble for himself because of his blackmailing the local companies with the pollution evidence collected against them. At least so was he accused at the local court, which spelled trouble for Shanshan too. Jiang was sentenced for more than ten years, but she did not leave him at that time, as you know.'

'Yes, I know the part concerning the blackmail in the name of the consulting fee, as claimed by the local government, even though he did work as an environmental consultant at the time, and people paid him as a matter of course.'

'But I don't think she knew what you had done for her, so brilliantly, and so generously, I have to say. Even today, she still has no clue about it. Nevertheless, it might have turned out to be just as well.'

What Huang meant by 'just as well', Chen understood. The young cop had persisted in seeing Shanshan as a potential troublemaker, not a match politically suitable for the chief inspector, a star with a promising prospect in the Party system.

In fact, Shanshan herself had given the same reason for choosing to part with him, but he had always wondered whether there was such 'a promising prospect' for him in the Party system.

Not too long ago, he had published an article in *Guangming Daily*, speaking in favor of the judicial independence, which was soon criticized by someone high above as the proof of his advocating the Western system. Zhao, too, had chastized him in an unusually serious manner. In fact, his very survival in the system remained open to question. His recent exclusion from the serial murder investigation spoke volumes about it too. But he saw no point discussing it with Huang.

Things were changing so fast, so unpredictably, like in the two lines written by the poet Du Fu in the Tang dynasty:

> *The cloud looks now like a white blouse,*
> *but the next moment, like a black retriever.*

Shanshan, a young, idealistic but helpless environmental engineer at the time of their meeting in Wuxi, was now a celebrated activist or 'public intellectual' with millions of followers online.

And at the same time, a Big Buck's wife, too.

But that was something puzzling him as well. If a politically incorrect troublemaker – the way Huang saw her – was unsuitable for the chief inspector, she would have made an equally unacceptable match for a Big Buck, who had to make money by maintaining good relationships with the government. And possibly even worse, for she was now considered as one potentially threatening to the Party regime.

Is that how Zhao came to request Chen's service?

'Are you still there, Chief Inspector Chen?'

Huang's anxious voice pulled him back to the present moment, which was increasingly suffocating in the public phone booth.

'Yes, I'm here. Sorry, I've just thought of something else

in the case. Please find out as much as possible about Shanshan, both in the past and the present. And about the people related to her, too. I don't know what info concerning her is truly relevant at this stage. Call me at this number,' Chen said, reading out the number of the new SIM card purchased at the convenience store. 'Make sure that you contact me at this number only. And you should have a special number too.'

'No problem, when I call you again, you'll have my new number.'

Inspector Chen must have spent quite a long time in the booth. It was perhaps not a common sight in today's Shanghai. He thought he'd better leave.

Walking out, he moved along the bank again, looking around like a traveler lost in thought.

There was a tiny, ungainly sampan moving on the river, a rare scene against the background of the increasingly metropolitan city.

It was several years earlier – or just yesterday, as it seemed to him at the moment – that he had learned about the seriousness of the environmental crisis, and much more, particularly about what was behind the crisis, in Shanshan's company in a boat drifting on the lake.

And it was also in her company that he had composed the poem, which Zhao had read without knowing that those lines had come to Chen in the sleepless night, with her nestling against him in the shabby dorm room, her bare shoulder rippling like the lake water under the clear Wuxi stars. It was such a passionate, creative impulse as he had not since experienced.

For the moment, what kept pushing back to his mind was, however, an indelible image of her debunking his naïve imagination on the lake.

That afternoon, the two of them had huddled together in a sampan on the dirty green algae-covered water expanse where he was so intoxicated with her closeness that he began mumbling exaggerated lines about the 'poetic moment', with her bare feet on his lap . . .

Then she did something totally unexpected to him. She shifted to the side and put her feet into the water.

He did not know why she suddenly chose to dabble her bare feet there, her white ankles flashing above the darksome smelling water. He leaned over, her long black hair straying across his cheek. Watching, he wondered whether he should do the same, bending over to undo his shoelaces. But she was already pulling out of the water, her feet covered with a layer of green grime, as if painted, still wet, slimy, sticky . . .

'Do you want to call that poetic?'

'You don't have to do that, Shanshan.'

But he failed to juxtapose these remembered images by the lake, no matter how hard he tried, with the one falling out of the folder from Zhao – a mature yet strikingly beautiful activist fighting for her idealistic cause.

How Shanshan had turned into Yuan Jing was a metamorphosis beyond imagination, though anything was possible in 'the socialism with China's characteristics'.

He wanted to take the picture out of the folder again, but he checked himself. There was a job waiting for him. 'An important job', not just for Zhao, but also for himself, for Shanshan.

And for those dreams he had cherished when writing that poem beside her.

He had to turn himself into a detached, determined cop. There were things he had to do, though he was not sure how helpful they could be.

So he headed to the subway station.

As he was coming into view of the station, he slowed down to a stop again.

This time he took out his white cellphone and dialed the number of Peiqin, Detective Yu's wife.

'I've been such a long admiring customer of your noodles, Peiqin. Shanghai's Number One Noodles, as I've always said,' he said in a hurry, without mentioning his own name. 'Now I would like to order ten *Zongzi* – the palm-leaf-wrapped sticky rice with pork stuffing; another must from your restaurant that people have told me is wonderful. You know my place, and please deliver it today. Here is my new phone number. Your delivery people will need it.'

'Shanghai's Number One Noodles' was an exaggeration for Peiqin's restaurant. As far as he knew, nobody else had raved about her culinary skills like that. So it was a joking comment known only to the two of them. He believed she would get the message *behind* the message.

'Oh yes, the delivery people shall need it,' Peiqin too said in a hurry without bringing up his name, as expected. 'Please go ahead and give the number to me.'

'It's the number I'm calling you with today. A new one I've just acquired.'

'Thanks, our loyal customer. A basket of *Zongzi* shall be on the way to your apartment soon. Don't worry about it. Your satisfaction is guaranteed.'

'Thanks!'

It was around three that Detective Yu walked Peiqin out of the Shanghai Police Bureau.

Her visit with a small bamboo basket of *Zongzi* had been a total surprise, though perhaps not so with some of his colleagues. She had brought him delicacies there before. With the Dragon Festival drawing nearer, *Zongzi* was seasonally fashionable.

But with his colleagues surrounding the basket, Yu did not have the chance to ask Peiqin about the real purpose of her unannounced visit.

It was not until she stepped out of the bureau that Peiqin took his hand, like the loving wife she was, and pressed a small piece of paper against his palm.

'His new cell number,' she whispered, her lips touching his cheek.

'I see.'

The message from her was unmistakable. Inspector Chen must have had something that alarmed him. He had gone out of his way to have Peiqin bring the new number to Yu, worrying about people tapping into their phone conversation.

Again, Peiqin had proved herself to be 'an extraordinary wife to a cop', as Chen had said of her. In addition to Chen's new number, she also brought Yu an old, out-of-fashion cell-phone left at home by Qinqin, who was using a new iPhone in school.

'On the way to the bureau, I bought a SIM card for you, under my name,' she said. 'So you don't have to worry.'

He did not raise any questions about all the secrecy.

'I was just talking to Detective Qin about a sex video posted online—'

But another cop came walking out of the bureau, waving his hand at the couple at the gate.

'Come back home early for dinner.' Peiqin left without saying anything else. They would talk more in the evening. He hugged her awkwardly on the street corner.

After parting with her, Yu lit a cigarette and took out that old phone left by Qinqin.

'Hello, who's calling?'

Chen must have been surprised at the unknown number on the screen.

'It's me. The manager of Shanghai's Number One Noodles has just come over with a basket of *Zongzi*. And my new number, too. What's up, Chief?'

'She has delivered fast. So thoughtful of her!' Chen went on after a short pause. 'To begin with, I'm officially off the case in the bureau. Comrade Secretary Zhao from Beijing wants me to check into something else.'

'Wow, another important assignment from Zhao. Then you don't have to worry about the case in the bureau. And it might be just as well. I simply cannot stand the company of Li and Qin. They did not want to give the case to us, but now it's too much for them.'

'Don't worry about them. We just do what we are supposed to do.'

'If the case is solved, it's to the credit of the Homicide squad. But if not, they'll find one way or another to blame us for it, particularly you. Why should we bother?'

'Come on. Our special case group is really under your charge. We cannot afford to look on with our arms crossed when a serial murderer is still at large.'

'But you're officially off the case.'

'I don't think I have to be doing Zhao's job every minute of the day. It's just that I don't have to tell others about it. Anything new about the case?'

'The latest development is mainly about a sex video of Xiang and her husband Vice Mayor Geng posted online. That's why Internal Security and Qin joined forces in a hurry. They've come under so much pressure.'

'A sex video of the two! Give me some more details.'

'Sorry, not that much from me. Qin talks like an old tooth already loose yet still hanging on in there. You have to shake it real hard, but it won't come out totally. The video was taken before their marriage. She wasn't a journalist at the time. That's about all I've got from him.'

'She's new at *Wenhui*?'

'Yes, Xiang came to *Wenhui* about a year ago. One day after her death, a sex video of her and Geng broke out online. Unbelievably graphic, it instantly turned into a sensational scandal. Geng passed out because of it.'

'Not just because of her death, I see. But I don't think I've met her at *Wenhui* before.'

'Guess what Detective Qin said to me. "Chief Inspector Chen has so many good friends in the newspaper, he's surely able to find out more about her."'

'No, I'm not supposed to be involved in the investigation – whether through my connections in the newspaper or not,' Chen said deliberately. 'Incidentally, you or Peiqin may know someone there too.'

'Who?'

'Lianping, the *Wenhui* journalist who came to the Buddhist service for Peiqin's parents.'

'Yes, I remember, now you mention it. Peiqin met with her again for something else after that service.'

'And Lianping went out of her way to help – through Peiqin.' Chen added in spite of himself, 'She's now happily married with a baby on the way.'

'I see.' Yu abruptly changed the subject. 'Xiang's case has several things in common with the previous three. In the early morning. In the center of the city – the fourth one happened on the corner of Weihai and Shanxi Roads, which is still quite a central location. And a fatal hammer blow from behind. After the meeting, Qin spoke with Internal Security again.'

'It would have been too much of a coincidence for Xiang not to be part of the serial murder case—'

At that point Yu saw two cops moving toward him. One of them knew Yu quite well.

'Sorry, I'll talk to you later, our number one loyal customer.'

Fifteen minutes later Inspector Chen got back to his apartment, still disturbed about the phone call from Detective Yu.

Yu must have had his reason to cut short the phone call. Chen was not worried about that, but the growing complications around the Xiang case would make it a tough one for Yu. In spite of his grumbling, Chen knew Yu would not hesitate to throw himself headlong into the investigation.

For the moment, however, there was nothing Chen could possibly do to help until he had more information – reliable information – available from the bureau.

But how was he going to really help while he also had the Shanshan investigation on his hands?

Looking up, he found the smoggy sky over Puxi, west of the river, more somber than over Pudong, east of the river.

He made a pot of extra strong black coffee, poured out a cup for himself, and gazed out the window for several minutes absentmindedly.

A black bird came circling out of nowhere, flapping its wings furiously above the window. In the folk superstition, it might have served as another ominous sign – for the assignment from Zhao?

For the serial murder investigation?

Or for both of them?

He remained inexplicably disturbed, though he did not believe in signs.

Then he turned on the computer and started research on the Internet about the air pollution.

The issue of horrible air quality in China had a fairly long history, but for so many years after 1949 people had paid no attention to it because of their living in a 'closed China' under

Mao, and 'everything's all right' in the Party-controlled media. After the ending of the Cultural Revolution, the economic reform launched by Deng Xiaoping began to bring about dramatic changes for the country. China witnessed itself relentlessly consumed in construction and urbanization at a breakneck speed, and the air problem grew worse and worse, what with modern and ultramodern high-rises shooting up like bamboo roots after a spring rain, looming here and there and blocking out the sky, with a growing number of cars and air conditioning everywhere, with the ever-increasing-and-worsening carbon emission like the genie out of the bottle, and with industrial pollution further deteriorating and expanding.

He was getting depressed with his reading, heaving a long sigh, when the cellphone started to shriek, all of a sudden, like a siren breaking into the dark recesses of his thoughts.

The phone screen presented a chart showing PM 2.5 at an alarmingly high level, and a message underneath warning people of all ages not to go out unless absolutely necessary.

Staring at the message for a minute or two, he plunged himself back into the cyber maze of information. This time, he thought of something mentioned by Zhao at the hotel, and tried something new, putting various combinations of key words into the new search effort. As he put in 'air pollution' together with 'America', a number of articles popped up.

As it turned out, one of the earliest acknowledgements of the serious problem came out of the American Embassy in Beijing, at least according to an article that explored the issue from the very beginning.

Despite the invariable description of China's air as 'light-hearted blue' in the People's Daily, *people began to be more and more bothered with the oppressive black smoggy mass before their own eyes. With more information accessible through the Internet, they also realized the air quality might not necessarily be the same elsewhere in the world. Things finally came to a head when posts appeared online, quoting the US Embassy Twitter feed that tracked air pollution in Beijing, and its number of followers was rapidly multiplied by* Weibo. *To their shock,*

*people learned that on the day the level of PM 2.5 – the
Particulate Matter less than 2.5 micrometers in size in
the air – was marked in the Embassy monitor as
'unhealthy for sensitive groups', the air quality was still
categorized as 'excellent' by the Beijing Environmental
Bureau. It was actually made possible by excluding the
level of PM 2.5, which was condemned by the Party
officials as unheard of, unscientific, and unacceptable to
China. In short, the American Embassy was accused of
making something out of nothing – out of thin air.*

*At a press briefing, the Chinese Foreign Ministry
spokesman went so far as to demand foreign embassies
stop publishing their reports on air quality. He criticized the reports as illegal and irresponsible, and
declared that the Beijing government alone should be
authorized to monitor and publish the air quality information. In conclusion, he called for the Chinese people
to trust the great and glorious Party, to repudiate the
malicious misinformation as reported by the American
Embassy.*

*What's so face-losing for the Party authorities, the
patriotism propaganda proved to be an utter failure.
Almost unanimously people chose to believe the monitor in
the American Embassy instead. It's not too surprising
in the days when they could not drink clean water, breathe
fresh air, and see the azure sky. On the Internet, distrust
of official air quality statistics started up like the unstop-
pable cacophony of cicadas in the summer, cutting
through the firewalls of the frenzied governmental cyber
control. It shook up the appearance of a 'harmonious,
prosperous society' under the Party's regime, which was
undergoing a credibility bankruptcy. The people were
sick and tired of the repeated ridiculous cover-up orchestrated from above . . .*

Reading on, Chen wondered how that article could have
survived online with the net cops patrolling around all the
time. Then he noted that it was an article originally posted
a couple of years earlier. Somebody must have saved it as a

Word document and reposted it with the latest waves of toxic air overwhelming the country again. The reposted article would most likely be blocked soon. He printed out a hard copy and saved it to a file in his own computer as well.

Clicking on the mouse, he came upon another related *Weibo* post, which read like a sequence to the earlier one. Apparently, it was one of the most heated topics on the Internet.

> *Indeed, China is in an environmental crisis, a result of the GDP-oriented economic development and of the one-Party system corruption, for which people are now paying a terrible price.*
>
> *The debate about the 'American air quality monitor' drew angry protests from the Chinese people. They condemned the government spokesman, comparing him to a thief in an ancient Chinese proverb – one who stuffs his own ears in the act of stealing a bell while hoping that others may not be able to hear anything just like him. In the last analysis, the clean air being so essential to people's daily life, you cannot simply say, 'Hold your breath, China.' In a* Weibo *cartoon, underneath a picture of the Beijing spokesman's solemn face, a netizen commented: 'To say in the Beijing dialect, he just asks for a slap on the face.'*
>
> *It did not take that long for the authorities to include, however reluctantly, the PM 2.5 level as part of the official air quality index. Needless to say, the same spokesman was now busy producing the reasons why it's an officially acknowledged part of the index, rather than the unscientific fabrication on the part of the American Embassy . . .*

Taking a deep breath, Chen bookmarked it along with several other posts. He might have to reread them more closely, he thought, with the onset of a dull headache, when he heard a light knock on the door.

It was a young delivery man carrying a small basket of *Zongzi*, speaking to Inspector Chen with a strong Shandong accent. '*Zongzi* for you, sir. Cooked this afternoon, still warm.'

The food delivery too was something new, fashionable in the city – everything possible for delivery to the door.

With more and more people pouring into Shanghai from other provinces, delivery services became a new industry with job opportunities for them. To start up, they just needed a bike or an electronic bike, piling up a variety of delivery goods behind them like acrobats, cutting through the lanes of traffic throughout the city. It was a great convenience to some consumers, who, instead of going out to restaurants, would simply take out their smartphones, click the order on such websites as *Are You Hungry* or *Time to Eat*, and their delicacies would come to the door in twenty minutes.

Chen had a mixed feeling, however, about the food delivery service. Perhaps he was just too old-fashioned. For him, delicacies had to be served fresh and hot. With delivery like that, no matter how fast, the taste could not be the same.

Besides, the plastic containers and bags used in the delivery service – particularly with such huge demand – could be a horrible ecological waste.

But it was a different story with the *Zongzi* from Peiqin. She was just so thoughtful, even though she knew he had mentioned it as an excuse in the phone call.

In addition, there was a printout with a short sentence: 'Anything else I can do?' Beneath it, a number of web links. She apparently wanted him to check these.

He gave the delivery man a tip.

After unwrapping a *Zongzi* into a bowl and picking up the laptop, Inspector Chen stepped out to the balcony despite the bad air. Having skipped lunch, he was hungry.

The stuffing of pork belly and salted egg yolk in the *Zongzi* tasted surprisingly savory, blending different textures and flavors miraculously, and the soy-sauce-soaked sticky rice proved to be no less satisfying. He could not help beginning to unwrap another *Zongzi*.

The electronic links turned out to be a different surprise.

None of them showed any content apart from a note saying that 'the post is in violation of the government regulation, so it is deleted'.

Peiqin must have collected the list in a hurry. Judging by the wording in the links, they could have been about a video posted online, or stories about it.

Then it came to his realization. The links to the sex video concerning Xiang and Geng.

If so, they might still have been viewable at the time Peiqin compiled the list, but shortly afterward they were all deleted by the net cops, who could do anything and everything in the name of fighting 'violation against the government regulation'.

But such a speed in itself spoke about the political sensitivity of the video. Otherwise it would not have been blocked so quickly.

So there was nothing else for Chen to do about the video – at least not at the moment. Taking out a cigarette, he put it back into the pack.

He decided to go on with the research around the assignment from Zhao.

It could be a different approach, he contemplated, to start by sorting out what Zhao had said to him in the light of the newly conducted online research.

Among the things highlighted in his mind was Zhao's mention of Shanshan's recent trip to the United States. That now made much more sense. The official media had repeatedly tried to blame the people's complaining about the air pollution on the American propaganda conspiracy, of which Shanshan's trip could have been easily interpreted as an integrated part.

But with the existence of PM 2.5 in the air finally acknowledged in China, putting Shanshan and America together could backfire, serving as a reminder of the Party propaganda fiasco.

Another highlight concerned Shanshan's office in Shanghai. The information contained in the folder from Zhao provided no specific clues, except that the office was located at a high-end area in Shanghai, on Huaihai Road close to the New World. An expensive office under her name for more than one year. Why? She was anything but materialistic, as far as he remembered. With such a widespread community complaining and protesting about the pollution, she could have been really busy with a variety of activities as a 'public intellectual', working with a considerable number of her associates and visitors at the office, including some influential Big Bucks in the city of Shanghai, as Zhao had emphatically put it. During all that time, however, she had not tried to contact him – not once. It could have been much easier for her to learn things about him in Shanghai, with news about his work available from time to time in the local newspapers.

Still, he thought he was able to guess the reason why she had chosen not to do so, though there could have been hundreds of other reasons, which remained unknown or inexplicable to the befuddled inspector, and unpleasant for him to speculate on.

He pulled himself together for the other puzzling emphases in Zhao's talk, particularly about his familiarity as a native Shanghainese with the city and its people, and in addition, with the contaminated Tai Lake as the author of the poem. It did not add up for Zhao to give him the job for those reasons.

Could it be possible that the stakes for the investigation – whatever or whoever got involved – were so high that Zhao had to request his service so obliquely instead of telling him the true reason?

Whatever the scenarios, the inspector had to move ahead, floundering and struggling like the protagonist in the Beijing opera *Crossroads*, knowing not who's attacking who in the pitch-black night, flourishing his sword blindly.

It was out of the question for him to wait in uncertainty, doing nothing.

The night was spreading out against the sky, reminiscent of the cold, darksome water Shanshan and he had touched as she dabbled her feet in Tai Lake.

Finally back to the desk in the study, Inspector Chen was no longer hungry, having finished three *Zongzi* out on the balcony, yet he'd made no real progress whatsoever on the case except for another text message from Ouyang.

'I've just checked with our office assistant Nanhua. Two groups requested copies, both from Beijing. She's positive about that. One, the Party Central Discipline Committee, and the other, from some office in the China Petroleum Building, possibly related to the Ministry of Petroleum Industry.'

The request by Zhao was no news. But the inspector did not remember having anything to do with the people in the Petroleum Ministry. Why should they be interested in the poem?

In the hotel, Zhao had mentioned about his recommendation of the poem to some others in Beijing, who too could have requested copies as a result. That seemed to be a plausible interpretation, but not really a convincing one.

Then he recalled something else – albeit just a glance of it – about the petroleum industry in a document spread out on the desk in Zhao's hotel room.

'That's intriguing,' Chen texted back.

'Come and talk to her if you have some specific questions. She may be able to tell you more about it. Nanhua has prepared the copies of the magazine for you.'

It was just like Ouyang, meticulous about everything.

But what if Ouyang's message was intended as an urge for the inspector to approach Nanhua for more information about the petroleum industry? It had been criticized for its impact on air pollution.

He might have just been too paranoid of late, he tried to reassure himself, in connection with Shanshan.

'Thanks, Ouyang. I will. See you tomorrow.'

There was no point in continuing to cudgel his brains out in the dark. Exhausted, he felt more like a hollow man, his head filled with straw, with the shadow inevitably falling between the idea and the reality, and between the speculation and the action.

Out of the window, he glimpsed a faint light flickering in the distance, then vanishing. The room appeared so still, solitary, with nothing except the tick of the electric clock measuring the invisible yet the always present second moving into the past. The stars were staring down through the dark and murky sky, as if trying to whisper to him from a long-lost dream in which thousands of ships were sailing out in the silence of the night.

Was he being Eliotic again?

On a moment of impulse, he dug out the copy of *Shanghai Literature* and turned to the poem, in which he found himself moving with her with a real purpose – not at all like a hollow man.

Who is the one walking beside you?
Last night, a white water bird
flew into my dream again,
like a letter, telling me
that the pollution's under control –
I awoke to see the night cloud
breaking through the ether, thinking
with difficulty, shivering,
as if the prison cell key was
heard turning only for once
before the door opens
to the anemic stars lost
in the lake of the waste . . .

But is it Shanshan in real life, or Shanshan in Inspector Chen's imagination?

His head heavy, he tried to see in those lines the same Shanshan by the lake as the one in Zhao's description at the Pudong hotel, but with little success.

Detective Yu had something on his mind, which Peiqin saw clearly the moment he came home that evening.

'It must have been a busy day for you, Yu.'

'A tough day,' he grumbled.

'Take a break first. Dinner will be ready soon. I've brought back some cooked dishes from the restaurant. Among them, the fried small croak is your favorite.'

She knew he would soon start telling her about things in the bureau. She did not have to push. Whatever the problem, they should have dinner first. It was already quite a late dinner for them.

About half a year ago, Peiqin and Yu had been to a school reunion in which those 'ex-educated youths' agreed unanimously that things for Yu and Peiqin were more than acceptable, practically enviable. With the decent pay from Yu's job in the bureau, and with the fairly good income from her job in the state-run restaurant as well as from her private-run eatery, and with their son Qinqin doing great in college, she too thought she had hardly anything to complain about. Their generation was usually called a 'wasted generation'. Yet despite ten years wasted in the countryside of Yunnan Province as 'educated youths', and with their opportunities for any real education like Qinqin's lost, things had turned out to be relatively fine for the two of them.

Of late, however, there was something vaguely bothering her. After these years, she was ready to slow down a little into 'the autumn of life', like that described in books, but Yu remained restless. Not that it was easy for him to be relaxed, Peiqin understood, with his work involving life and death for people, but she also suspected another reason.

Yu was fond of saying, 'Working with Inspector Chen has been one of the best things to happen to me,' with which she mostly agreed. He appeared to be quite content to play the second fiddle to Chen, who was not just his boss, but also his partner and friend. However, Chen was such a restless one, which must have infected Yu.

So she prepared a special dinner, which might unwind him a bit. With their son Qinqin studying and working part-time in college, it was going to be a peaceful night for just the two of them. They could talk, and not just about the new case in his bureau.

On the dining table she had bamboo shoots braised in soy sauce, and wok-fried small croakers. Both were his favorites. She also had a bowl of hot and sour soup of tofu, egg and minor mill. A new recipe she had learned from a short story by a rediscovered writer named Wang Zengqi. For a change, she put on the table a bottle of Qingdao, and slices of a thousand-year egg as well as peanuts in saltwater as the cold dishes for the beer.

'I'll have a sip with you this evening, Yu. Our small restaurant has been doing great. Its revenue has surpassed a hundred thousand yuan this month.'

'That's something calling for celebration.'

Yu finished his cup of beer in three or four gulps. His mood seemed to have improved by the time she served the hot dishes and soup on the table. Sure enough, he opened up.

'Like in an old proverb, the roof must get leaky again when it rains so hard,' he started.

Of late, Yu had come to talk more and more like his father, Old Hunter, who was in the habit of frequently quoting proverbs as a prelude to the talk.

'Don't talk too much about your case over the meal. It won't help with digestion,' she said, smiling a knowing smile, adding another piece of bamboo shoot to his bowl.

Nothing's like a good meal at home, she believed.

When Yu finished the last piece of fried small croaker with a satisfied sigh, Peiqin rose to clear the table. He tried to help, but she stopped him.

'You just enjoy a cup of tea inside. I'll join you in a minute or two.'

It was a fairly warm spring. When she stepped into the bedroom, he was sitting propped against a couple of pillows, holding a folder in one hand, hurrying to stub out a cigarette in the other. No teacup on the nightstand. For once, she chose not to say anything about it.

'Another tough case for your squad, I guess, the way your inspector called me about the Shanghai Number One Noodles,' she said instead, changing into a florid cloth robe she had made for herself in imitation of the fold-on style she had seen in her 'educated youth' years in Yunnan Province. The Dai minority women there made their robes like that. Memories of those years still lingered.

'It's not a case for our squad, but a tough one. In all appearances, it's a serial murder case.'

'Now tell me about it.' She moved to sit beside him on the bed, taking up his hand as if examining the nicotine stain on his finger. 'This afternoon you mentioned a video scandal online. I made a list of possible links to it in the restaurant – for you and for Chen. But when I tried to look into them, the content disappeared.'

'No, I could not find any of them, either. But I'm not really surprised, I mean, at the disappearance of those posts.'

She slid in beside him under the large towel blanket. He draped an arm over her shoulder, like always, before telling her about things discussed in the bureau.

'For a case not under the charge of your squad, you don't have to worry too much,' she said softly. 'Just like in one of your father's favorite proverbs: "People are not supposed to cook in other people's kitchen."'

'But according to Chen, with the date of the opening session of the People's Congress drawing nearer, Li wants us to help and have the case solved as soon as possible. He's now anxious for others to work in the kitchen.

'What's more, the murderer will strike again, possibly in another week – actually less than a week with two days already gone. Qin and his squad have wasted more than three weeks without getting anywhere. No clue to the identity of the murderer, nor any idea as to where he will pounce on the next prey.'

'What about Chen's take on the situation?'

'He has little doubt about it being a serial murder, so the murderer will go on killing – one victim a week until we catch him. But Chen was snatched away in the middle of the case discussion this morning.'

'Snatched away – what do you mean?'

'Zhao, the retired first secretary of the Party Central Discipline Committee, called into the bureau out of the blue, requesting his service for something else. Something so confidential our Party Secretary Li dared not ask any questions about it, let alone say no.'

'But it may not be too bad for Chen. At least there's still someone from the Forbidden City who trusts him. No wonder he contacted me in such a stealthy way. Another highly sensitive case, I bet.'

'That I don't know, but it's quite likely. That's why he gave you the new number in the coded message. But what about our serial murder case in the bureaus?'

'What are you planning to do?'

'Nothing but the routine canvassing. Perhaps there're some connection overlooked in the folder Qin has just given me. For Li, the Party's interest has to be placed above everything, so he will not have it declared a serial murder case at this moment, lest the city is thrown into a collective panic. But if another victim turns up, and then another still, it means big trouble for the bureau, and for him—'

A text message came in from Chen. Glancing at it, Yu frowned.

'Chen's going to Wuxi. Another mysterious trip.'

'To Wuxi? There was a murder case he investigated there, I remember, several years ago.'

'No, he had a vacation there – an all-inclusive package Zhao gave him for free, he told me, as the lake was terribly contaminated that year. He helped a local young cop there with an investigation without taking any credit. That criminal was caught and punished. I don't think the present trip of his is related to that in any way.'

'Well, he tells you whatever he chooses,' Peiqin said, slightly shaking her head. 'But during the investigation he was devastated with an ill-starred romantic affair.'

'How did you know? He never talked to me about it.'

'You're a good detective, but you're unable to detect those things with your inspector.' She jumped down barefoot to take a copy of *Shanghai Literature* from a small corner shelf. 'He's written a long poem about the experience. I happened to read it in the magazine.'

'A love poem?'

'No, not exactly. She's an environmental activist or something like that. But it's one written after his vacation there. He appeared not to be himself for several months after he came back. So do you think his trip to Wuxi may have anything to do with it?'

'No, not possible at this moment, not with Zhao's assignment on his hands.'

'Whatever you say. By the way, is there anything I could do to help? It's similar to the red mandarin dress serial murder case, I remember, about the bizarre revenge of a murderer traumatized during the Cultural Revolution.'

'Well, people are already discussing it online, according to Qin, about the possibility of the murderer killing another one anytime soon.'

'Then I'll have a busy day tomorrow,' she said with a knowing smile, 'to get some info on the Internet before they're blocked. I think I know a way or two to climb over the wall.'

'The firewall, you mean?'

'Yes.'

'No need to put yourself in too much risk. It's not even a case for our squad. You're just so busy with your things in the restaurant.'

'Hasn't your chief inspector called me the best amateur female investigator?'

'Now you mention it, he actually referred to you in a phone call today.'

'What's that?'

'Remember the *Wenhui* journalist who came with him to the Buddhist service at Longhua Temple?'

'Lianping, that's her name. A young, vivacious girl. What about her?'

'The fourth victim, also a young girl named Xiang, used to work in the same newspaper office. Chen mentioned that you knew Lianping.'

'Yes, she once tried to help out, provide some information through me. So he wants me to contact her?'

'He did not say so, but we hardly know anything about Xiang.'

'Lianping will be more than willing to help again, I bet.'

'How can you be so sure of it?'

'You men never see what's going on before your very eyes.' Peiqin nestled closer to put a finger lightly on his eyelid. 'Not because of me, needless to say, but because of your chief inspector.'

For Inspector Chen, it never rains but it pours.

Fifteen minutes to ten that evening, a text message came in from Qin.

'We've just got some latest info about the last victim. Shall I have it specially delivered to you, Chief Inspector Chen?'

'Thanks. But the assignment from Comrade Secretary Zhao will hardly leave me any time, I'm afraid.'

On second thought, he typed another sentence to Qin. 'I'll

touch base with you or with Detective Yu if I can manage to have some time tomorrow.'

It was quite likely nothing but a gesture on the part of Qin, but Chen thought he did not have to say something like a downright no.

And he was hungry again. So he unwrapped another *Zongzi* and put it in the microwave. To his surprise, it tasted even more delicious when warmed, with its stuffing a unique combination of pork belly and Jinhua ham he had never tasted before.

As he rose from the table, licking the sticky-rice-covered forefinger, another unexpected ding broke into the silence of the night.

It was a text message from Huang to Chen's special phone.

'Got something for you.'

It was short and vague, carrying the implication that it could be something too sensitive for Huang to say, even on the special phone.

Taking a gulp of the cold coffee left in the cup, Chen thought he knew what he was going to do.

Like in *The Thirty-Six Stratagems*: to sail across the ocean undetected by the eyes in the sky.

After sending a response to Huang about his coming to Wuxi the next morning, he decided to compose a text message to Zhao. It did not have to be long or specific, which was one good thing about text messaging.

'Some possible new development. Going to Wuxi tomorrow – possibly for a day or two there.'

It appeared to be a plausible move, making sense for him to go to Wuxi, as it was from Wuxi that Shanshan came to Shanghai. No one would have to guarantee any breakthrough from the trip.

In the meantime, he might be able to do something else. For an investigation in secret like that, any 'new development' could reasonably justify his maneuvering around.

After pacing about in the room for several minutes, he worked out another short message to Zhao.

'Started to check around. Prepared to close in. For the moment, what I've learned so far seems to point to the petroleum industry – some office there in Beijing.'

The petroleum industry was commonly known to have a lot to do with the air pollution. For Shanshan's project, it might have been a matter of course for her to check into it. Anyway, it would probably not be a shot too wide of the mark. At this stage, he did not have to finger-point to anyone in specific.

But it demonstrated that he was carrying out Zhao's order in earnest.

DAY TWO
TUESDAY

Early the next morning, Chen sat dozing against the window of the high-speed Shanghai–Wuxi train, having slept only about three hours last night.

The train was already slowing down, with the LCD panel in the upper front of the car declaring: 'We are reaching Wuxi, the destination of the journey, in three minutes.'

It took less than an hour for the high-speed train to make the trip. China had indeed been changing so fast, as Zhao had put it. The last time he had traveled to Wuxi it took more than three hours.

He stepped down onto the platform where he saw Detective Huang running over waving his hand. Huang looked overjoyed at the sight of him.

'Chief Inspector Chen—'

'Call me Chen,' he said, raising a finger to his lips.

'I've arranged for a perfect stay at a fancy hotel with the lake view for "Master Chen" in Wuxi, Master Chen—'

'Just Chen, no Master. And I'm sorry to tell you that there's an unexpected change in the plan. I can spend only a couple of hours in Wuxi.'

'But I have already booked the hotel, Chen. A five-star one by the lake, and a gourmet reception dinner too. The chef will serve all the lake specials.'

'Thanks, Huang. I really appreciate it. Let's go to the hotel then. I'll check in under my name, but then you can stay there. For a couple of days more if you like. I'll give my credit card to the front desk. You don't have to worry about the expense, which is covered by the Party Central Discipline Committee. Afterward, you just need to mail the receipt to me.'

'I . . . I see, Chief Inspector Chen,' Huang said, unable to contain his excitement as he led Chen to a black Camry in the parking lot. 'Another big case from the Party Central Discipline Committee, I suppose.'

'It could be really big,' Chen said, seating himself in the front seat beside Huang. 'At this moment, I'm the officially designated tourist guide for Comrade Secretary Zhao during his vacation in Shanghai.'

'Wow, Comrade Secretary Zhao from Beijing. You don't have to explain any details to me, I totally understand. Just tell me what you want me to do. My lips are sealed.'

'You told me you have something for me – regarding Shanshan, right?'

'Right, I'll show them to you when we get to the hotel,' Huang said, pulling the car out into the avenue in front of the station. 'But let me tell you something about her first.'

'Go ahead, Little Huang.'

'To begin with, you remember the reason why she did not want to dump Jiang at that time, don't you?'

'Yes.'

'It's because of their common environmental cause, and all that idealistic stuff. To be fair to her, it's also because of her unwillingness to throw in the rock when Jiang's already at the bottom of the well.'

'Yes, that part I do remember.'

'Shortly after Jiang was thrown into jail, an article appeared in *Wuxi Daily* as some netizens maintained that he was innocent. In response, the article presented a long list of his wrongdoings, including his blackmail in the name of environment protection, and his extramarital affair with Shanshan, too. At the time he was seeing her, he was still not divorced from his wife. Shanshan was not named in the article, but with her factory and her position as an environmental engineer mentioned in the article, people knew it was her. I learned from my sources, however, she had no idea at the time about his marital status – not until the publication of the article. She was too upset at the discovery to go on with him.'

'That's really too much for her. You have uncovered the true reason. Good work.'

Ironically, it was also something that could have mattered

crucially to Chen, and to Shanshan as well, at the time of the inspector's vacation in Wuxi.

She could have made a different decision.

But not any more.

Huang might have noticed the change in his expression. For the next few minutes, Huang seemed to be concentrating on driving, saying nothing.

Chen did not speak, either.

Then the car was getting off the highway and coming into view of a new magnificent hotel at the lakeside. The hotel was appropriately named Wuxi Lakeside.

After they checked in with Chen's ID and moved into a spacious room, Huang produced a bunch of pictures in an envelope from his jacket pocket and spread them out on the desk like a colorful mosaic, shaking his head almost imperceptibly.

The pictures were of Shanshan – and Shanshan with a man – on a white sand beach stretching out to the blue horizon: some with them wandering along hand in hand, some with them sunbathing on the beach nestling against each other. Presumably they were on a vacation somewhere, with two or three resort signs visible in the distant background – in English.

'With her husband Yao in the United States.'

Following Huang's glance, Chen saw her in a white two-piece bikini in several pictures, and in two or three of them topless, lying on her stomach on a large florid beach towel, drawing her slender legs up backward, with Yao busy rubbing oil on her bare back.

There was almost a suggestion of them being from a tabloid magazine's exposé.

'Where did you get these pictures, Little Huang?'

'From Bei, the net cop I told you about in the phone call yesterday.' Huang added with a sheepish smile, 'I made fun of Bei about his monotonous work. Since Shanshan spends a lot of time in Shanghai and posts most of her blogs on big websites there, what's the point in your staring at her Internet posts all the time in Wuxi? You can hardly tell what she really looks like!'

'So you goaded him into telling things about her. A brilliant gambit.'

'Thank you, Chief Inspector Chen. I learned so much from you the last time you were in Wuxi. Anyway, Bei told me that he's busy communicating with cops in Shanghai and elsewhere. Even in Wuxi, he's responsible not just for her online writings. He can follow her everywhere in the Internet age. To prove his point, last night he sent me a large electronic file of pictures.'

'Unbelievable! How could she have shown these pictures to others?'

'I asked Bei the same question. He made no direct answer, but he added that you never know. No one can tell whether the pictures may come to appear online one of these days.'

'No, I don't think . . .' he said, leaving the sentence unfinished. Their appearance online might not give rise to a political scandal, like in a number of corruption cases, with the pictures provided by the enraged mistress or *ernai* dumped by the officials, but some controversy could be guaranteed. For these glamorous pictures of an attractive woman, an Internet celebrity barebacked and barelegged, in the company of a billionaire husband, touching and kissing each other, there would be far more voracious viewers than for her *Weibo* posts about the environmental crisis – they would be downloaded, forwarded and reforwarded, and most likely attract filthy comments, too.

'But some of these pictures could have been taken by her husband – in the United States or somewhere else out of China.'

'That I don't know. But if not, possibly by somebody else, without their knowledge,' Huang said, frowning. 'And according to Bei, that's just the latest bunch.'

'She's a celebrity with paparazzi following her around in the United States?'

'Or the pictures could have been taken by a surveillance camera—'

'On the beach?'

'That's a good point. It's hard to put a surveillance camera there. Not at a close range. But we don't have to worry too much about those pictures, Chief. They have nothing to do with us.'

'There is more than meets the eye, I'm afraid.'

'At least no hidden camera for this hotel room, I've made sure of that.'

'What else did Bei tell you?'

'Not much, but I think I'll talk to him again soon.'

'Don't push him too hard lest he gets suspicious,' Chen said, changing the subject as he rose, taking a look out the window. 'It's truly a nice hotel. It is called Li Lake here, right?'

'Yes, Li Lake is part of Tai Lake, a tributary. It's so named because the well-known statesman Fan Li stayed here more than two thousand years ago. The hotel is very close to Li Garden. Named after him. You can walk over there in just a couple of minutes.'

'You're right about that. Yes, Li Garden. Do you know about the romance of Fan Li and Xi Shi?'

'No, nothing. Except that Xi Shi was one of the four most famous beauties in ancient China.'

'Fan Li saved the State of Yue with his brilliant brain, and Xi Shi, with her voluptuous body. Afterward, the two lovers got reunited. As the King of Yue became so smug with the success, Fan Li and Xi Shi went into hiding, staying incognito in a house here with a back garden, and then sailing out on the lake in a sampan to no one knows where. It's said that they lived happily ever after.'

'Why?'

'According to a judgement made by Fan Li, the King of Yue, like other kings, was capable of sharing with others the hardship and travail, but not the fortune. Whether Fan Li and Xi Shi in their real lives were nearly as lucky as in the romantic tale, no one could tell. Such "happily-ever-after" stories are popular among Chinese people just because they're practically non-existent in reality.'

'You know more about Lake Li than a native Wuxianese, Chief Inspector Chen.'

'*O that I could retire by rivers and lakes, white-haired, sailing in a small boat after setting the country in order.*'

'What are you talking about?'

'Some lines by Li Shangyin, a Tang dynasty poet. Such wonderful lines about Fan Li.'

'You're a super scholar, Chief Inspector Chen.'

'Well, I'm just a tourist guide in Shanghai, so I need to know those stories. Now you go ahead and enjoy the five-star hotel, but I have to leave.'

'Whatever you say,' Huang said sheepishly. 'Take the set of pictures with you. I've printed them out for you.'

'Thanks. You're very considerate. The set could be a souvenir for the trip. Please forward an electronic file of the pictures to me too. I may have to enlarge some of them in case I need to study the details.'

In the Shanghai Police Bureau, Detective Yu was staring at a picture in a folder from Detective Qin.

Qin had dragged Yu over to his office first thing in the morning for a discussion on the latest development in the investigation. What Qin had just learned from Internal Security was vague, scanty, though the video about Xiang and Geng was developing into quite a storm in cyberspace.

'The video came out online late Saturday night or early Sunday morning, instantly going viral. Before it was blocked in less than five minutes, it had already been viewed for the Old Heaven alone knows how many times,' Qin said, shaking his head like a rattle drum. 'In connection with the serial murder case, an alarming number of wild conspiracy theories have popped up like the bamboo shoots after a heavy rain. Some of the netizens are simply like flies smelling blood, buzzing around non-stop.'

In spite of his requests, Internal Security refused to grant Qin full access to the video. All he got was that low-resolution picture presenting the intimate scene of Xiang and Geng holding each other in a massage room.

'But what could that possibly mean for our investigation, Qin?'

'For one thing, with the video posted online almost immediately after Xiang's death, it has further convinced Internal Security in their original theory about the case being a political one, as they have suspected from the beginning.'

'So they no longer take it as a possible part of the serial murder case?'

'They see no connection among the victims, the first three being ordinary people, and then Xiang in relation to Geng being anything but ordinary. They are bent on pushing forward in the political direction. It's being investigated as a deliberate attack against the Party image by making an example of a senior Party cadre like Geng.'

'Then it's not a case for our bureau.'

'No, they do not say so. They cannot afford to rule out the possibility of its being a serial murder case yet, but they do not share the information with us. Not even the video. The way they talked, they may have had some leads. At least that's the impression I've got. Anyway, Party Secretary Li is like an ant crawling on a hot wok, saying it's not just an ordinary serial murder case involving ordinary people.'

'Come on. No murder is an ordinary murder,' Yu said crossly. 'Any clue about the identity of the man who first posted the video online?'

'Believe it or not, it was put on a computer in an Internet bar with a fake ID. The owner of the Internet bar could only remember that it was a middle-aged customer wearing a large mask and amber-colored glasses, which seemed not to be something so suspicious in these smoggy days, and he left just about ten minutes later. The surveillance camera there only got a blurred picture of his back.'

'So it's been well planned. But here's a different question, Detective Qin. Xiang and Geng got married in spite of their age difference. The video about their intimacy in their prenuptial days – however graphic or pornographic – could only have been a huge embarrassment, but not an irrecoverable political disaster for him.'

'I've thought about the same question too. And the Internal Security officer named Lao refused to give me any relevant details in that aspect. "Too politically confidential!" That's about all Lao said to me. So how could it have led anywhere?'

'For a political case, the release of the video at this moment does not make much sense.'

'Could all the other killings have been something like the

preparation for this final one? With all the public attention drawn to the killings, the old man would have been landed in a really tight spot.'

Yu did not think he could rule out the possibility, but it was too far-fetched.

'Xiang was a pretty girl. It's possible that she had someone so enamored of her that when she threw herself into Geng's arms, he got hold of the video tape and released it online.'

'No, that does not add up. If that secret lover had been really such a romantic soul, how could he have chosen to post online that pornographic video about her writhing in another man's arms?'

'You have your point, Detective Qin. But let's not talk about Internal Security and the video for the moment. What are you going to do?'

'Well, let me ask you a question first, Detective Yu. Has Chief Inspector Chen discussed with you about the case?'

'Yes, he called me yesterday. He has been simply overwhelmed in Zhao's assignment. Don't ask me what it is. He did not tell me a single word about it. But he did promise he would help in whatever ways possible. With his permission, I took out that casebook of his on the red mandarin dress serial murder and studied it.'

'Yes, I remember that particular case.'

'According to his notes, for a serial murder case, it could be committed for some reason understandable to the criminal alone. Regarding the fourth victim, Xiang, we do not know enough at this stage, but for the first three, I've done some thinking by myself.'

'Please go on, Detective Yu.'

'In accordance with the file from you, there were no enemies known for Peng, the first victim – such a poor and pitiable woman – quite understandably with no one around harboring enough hatred to kill her. As for the ever-increasing medical disputes in today's society, people may be angry with doctors or nurses, but it does not make sense to target a night caregiver.

'And then for the second victim, Linghu, there's a similar problem. He had no known enemy or adversary. People may have a grudge against some anchormen, for fake news, shameless propaganda, or whatever, but not against a weather anchorman. Supposing he made incorrect forecasts which caused some inconvenience for the viewers, it would have been far from enough for them to kill. Besides, there're other people working overnight in the city government building, not just those from the weather bureau. Could that have been a matter of mistaken identity?

'The same could be said about Yan, the third victim. People are complaining about the soaring real estate prices. But she's just a salesperson at an agency, having no control about the price. Besides, Lujiazui is where she lived, quite far from the agency office in Zabei District. She could have been running there just before going to the office.'

'So what's your point, Detective Yu?'

'For the possible reasons against the victims, there's no common denominator, but there's got to be something there, some reasoning understandable only to his twisted mind.'

'From your inspector's notes again, but we have no idea whatsoever about the identity of the murderer.'

'According to Chen, the criminal may have left some "signature", which speaks about what's making sense only to him, and from which we may begin to have a profile of the murderer.'

'But where are the so-called signatures?' Qin said incredulously. 'For a possible profile, we may say he's not someone old, he's capable of moving around quickly, and of striking out forcibly.'

'And of observing the background minutely. In spite of all the surveillance cameras in those central locations, there's no picture of a suspect near the crime scene.'

'That's true.'

'As for the possible signature, I think I would begin by studying all the pictures of the four victims at the crime scenes.'

'Of course you may have all of them. In addition to the pictures we have taken, I've already requested pictures and tapes from the surveillance cameras in those areas. Some of them may be stored in the evidence room.' Qin then added, 'In the meantime, I'm going to have another discussion with Internal Security.'

*   *   *

The high-speed train was incredible, even more so in the first-class car.

With the train tickets sold out at Wuxi Station except for the first-class seats, Inspector Chen had not hesitated to purchase a first-class one back to Shanghai. The car was clean and comfortable, sporting leather-cushioned seats, free Wi-Fi, TV in front of each seat, and ample space for him to stretch out to sleep, though that was something perhaps furthest from his mind.

Sipping from a bottle of water, he found himself to be the only passenger in the car, which was helpful. He could do some quiet thinking by himself without having to talk to any other passengers.

The trip to Wuxi had actually yielded more questions than answers.

Still, one of the answers meant a lot to him – the reason why Shanshan had decided to leave Jiang.

As for her subsequent choice of Yao, Chen did not want to speculate. Yao was a successful businessman, capable of providing for her things like a vacation at a picturesque seaside resort in the United States. And for that matter, a high-end office for her in Shanghai too.

So why not? For years, things had been hard enough on her, and she deserved a change for the better.

And those pictures also posed questions for him to ponder over. They're not irrelevant, not like the way Huang brushed them off: '*They have nothing to do with us.*'

Who took the pictures?

For what purpose?

What's more, how did they come into net cop Bei's computer?

Zhao might not have been the only one who had been paying more than serious attention to Shanshan.

And then the offhand comment about the pictures made by net cop Bei – 'Who could tell they may pop up online one of these smoggy days?'

It was out of the question for her to have put them online. If so, who else?

These questions proved to be overwhelming. He was hardly

aware of the scenes receding and changing so fast out of the train window.

He became increasingly positive about one thing. Zhao's assignment would turn out to be far less 'simple' than he had said to the inspector in the Hyatt Hotel.

A call came in through his public cellphone, ringing abruptly into his thoughts. It was from Party Secretary Li of the Shanghai Police Bureau.

'You know what, Chief Inspector Chen? Comrade Secretary Zhao of the Party Central Discipline Committee has just called me, making his request of your help. It is the top priority for our bureau, of course, to cooperate with Comrade Secretary Zhao. So I have told others that you are engaged in a very special, very important investigation. No one will say anything about it if you don't come to the bureau this week or next.'

Chen listened without making an immediate response.

'But the city government has called us several times about the serial murder case. Both the Homicide squad and Detective Yu have been going all out for the investigation. You understand the timing of it.'

'Yes, it is just like the People's Congress Blue,' Chen blurted out.

It was a standing joke about the politics of the air quality. Bad for months or years, the smoggy sky would suddenly turn blue with white clouds sailing over the Tiananmen Square on the occasion of important political events, such as the opening session of National People's Congress. The Beijing government would go all out, sparing no cost, shutting down the traffic and chimneys to present a perfectly blue-sky background in all propaganda. Once the occasion was over, everything would go back to the smoggy norm.

'Oh, you mean that. That's the business of the environmental office. For us, it's far more direct and immediate. If it's truly a serial murder case, we may soon have another victim on our hands – in less than a week. And then another, if the case remains unsolved and the killing continues. Too much responsibility for us at this critical juncture.'

That was sounding, ironically, like a sweet revenge for Chen. Li had been trying hard to keep the case away from him. Now the table was turned, with the politics behind getting more serious. If the murderer went on killing, right into the session of the People's Congress, the news would spread all over social media. Then Li's career would be pretty much finished.

Li knew nothing about Chen's own crisis, of course.

'I could not say no to Comrade Secretary Zhao, you know that, Party Secretary Li. No way to excuse myself from his assignment.'

'His assignment is highly important, but perhaps not that urgent. You don't have to come back to the bureau full time. Talk to Qin whenever you happen to not be that busy.' Li went on with no response from Chen, 'We have already sent out our reserve force patrolling those politically sensitive areas. Quite a number of neighborhood committees there have been notified too. But you can never have too much prevention for a case like this.'

'That's true.'

'In the meantime, what else did Comrade Secretary Zhao discuss with you?' Li said, suddenly changing the topic. 'He trusts you so much, we all know that.'

'I know,' he said, realizing that might be another reason for this phone call, and that he was in no position to reveal anything about it. 'Comrade Secretary Zhao's been bothered with the terrible air quality in Beijing. So it's just like a fresh air vacation for him.'

'Yes, a senior Party leader like Zhao deserves a much-needed break from the smog in the capital. By the way,' Li switched the topic again, 'where are you now? A lot of noise in the background.'

'I'm . . . Hold on for one minute . . .'

A train attendant in a light blue uniform with a white embroidered apron was coming over, pushing a screeching cart full of well-known Wuxi local products across the aisle, hawking in a sweet voice. He covered the phone with his hand. No need for him to buy anything on the train. In about half an hour he would be back in Shanghai.

'Anything you would like to have, sir?' she said at a closer distance, smiling with engaging dimples – like the cardamom buds in early spring in a Tang poem – and offering him a package of dried noodlefish. 'Special product of Tai Lake, Wuxi. Excellent for making silver and gold omelet.'

With him being the only passenger in the first-class car, he found it hard not to buy something from her, but he pushed back the package of dried noodlefish. That once again reminded him of what Shanshan had said to him at their first meeting: even though the water quality of Tai Lake was said to have improved, the fish still wasn't worth eating. He failed to recall, however, whether he had tasted the noodlefish together with her by the lake.

'For yourself or for your people in Shanghai,' the young attendant said, smiling. 'Anything you like.'

He picked up a dainty bamboo basket of fried gluten balls, two boxes of steaks braised in Wuxi style, and a small box of dried tofu cubes in special soy sauce. Back in Shanghai, he would have the Wuxi specials delivered to his mother. In his childhood, his parents had used to bring back home these Wuxi products. He felt guilty about not having visited her for more than a week.

He paid the attendant for the purchases and she put them in a large white plastic gift bag for him.

'Chief Inspector Chen?' Li's voice came over the phone again.

'Sorry, Party Secretary Li. A train attendant was pushing the food cart over to me. I have just bought some Wuxi snacks for my mother.'

'What a filial son!' Li exclaimed. 'So you're making the trip to Wuxi?'

'It's just part of the assignment for Zhao. But I'm anything but a filial son, leaving her all alone in Shanghai, and I'm going to have the Wuxi dried tofu cubes for myself.'

'Enjoy the trip, and enjoy the Wuxi snack too. If your mother needs help, let us know. And whenever you are not that busy by the lake, give some help to your colleagues in Shanghai.'

'I will.'

'Then see you back in Shanghai soon. People are getting really worried.'

To Chen's perplexity, after having inquired about his

whereabouts, Li did not push hard for the purpose of his Wuxi trip. As for the last sentence, Chen thought he could detect a note of genuine worry in Li's voice.

The inspector still held the phone in his hand. With complimentary Wi-Fi in the first-class car, he did a little research online and copied the link to an article about things for a tourist to do, to eat and to see in Shanghai.

He sent it to Zhao with a short message.

'Having just talked with Party Secretary Li of the police bureau, I assured him about my doing the tourist guide job for you. And it's true, as you can see from the article attached. Here are some ideas for your vacation in Shanghai. Of course, any time you need me, or anything else you want me to do, just let me know.

'Given the air quality, however, it may not be a good idea to stay outside for too long. There are a number of excellent restaurants in Lujiazui, which are listed in the article. They are also very close to the hotel. You may try one of them.

'In the meantime, I'm going to try to locate some environmental activists associated with her.'

It took Chen less than an hour to get to the office of *Shanghai Literature* from the Shanghai railway station via the subway.

The office was housed in the magnificent mansion of the Shanghai Writers' Association on Julu Road. In the early 1950s, the Party government had taken the high-walled mansion from a 'black family' and turned it over to the association with offices of literature magazines and other institutions there related to the association.

Ouyang was not in the magazine office. Nanhua, the office assistant, gave him five copies of the issue in a large envelope.

But to his disappointment, she could hardly give him anything new or useful in addition to what Ouyang had already told him. Except that the address of the other requester of the magazine was an office suite on the twenty-fifth floor in the China Petroleum Building in Beijing. She failed to recall the name of the office, so she turned to the page in the logbook bearing the name and address of the receiver.

'Mrs Zhu Yi, Room 22–24, Floor 25th, China Petroleum Building, Beijing.'

China Petroleum Building housed China Petroleum Ministry, no question about it. As far as Nanhua knew, those skyscraping buildings usually rented out rooms or even floors to other offices or companies not necessarily related to the industry. It could take quite a while to check out what office Mrs Zhu Yi was working in. Nanhua had no idea as to how to begin such a search.

So it was no more than ten minutes later that Chen walked out of the magazine office carrying a large envelope containing five copies of *Shanghai Literature*.

Since he was in the building of the Shanghai Writers' Association, he thought he might as well drop into Qiang's office to say hi to the old man, and to express thanks to him for his work all these years in the association, from which Qiang was now going to retire.

Qiang was something of an enigma. As the head of its foreign liaison office, he was supposed to be the one capable of speaking English or some other foreign languages, knowledgeable about Western cultures and conventions. But that was far from the case. A man of few words in public, Qiang looked more like an old farmer who had recently moved into the city of Shanghai. And he was also dressed as such.

It was whispered, however, that Qiang was either closely related to someone in Internal Security, or a secret member. It was the sort of question few wanted to ask. Anyway, he had worked there for over thirty years as one trusted by the Party authorities, with his position untouchable at the sensitive office. For the last two or three years, he also had an assistant who interpreted or translated for him as more and more writers came to Shanghai from other countries. But he handled his job well, got along with the visiting writers as well as the local writers, and with Chen too.

The moment Chen stepped into the office, Qiang rose with a broad smile breaking out on his deep-lined face.

'I was thinking of calling you, Chief Inspector Chen.'

'Anything you need me to do, Director Qiang?'

'No, just long time no see. I'm going to retire next month, as you may know.'

'I know. Having just picked up some copies of *Shanghai Literature*, I'm here at your office and thought long time no see indeed, as you have said.'

'Yes, I've read your long poem about Tai Lake. A number of people have read it too. What have you been doing lately?'

'Nothing particular, just one assignment after another.'

'Any assignment from Comrade Secretary Zhao? He has a very high opinion of you. People all say. He is staying at the Hyatt in Pudong this time, I've just heard.'

He was taken aback by the directness of the question from Qiang, but for a man of Qiang's connections, it was not too astonishing for him to know about Zhao's unannounced vacation.

'Believe it or not, I'm having a different assignment for Comrade Secretary Zhao this time. A tourist guide for his fresh air vacation in Shanghai.'

'Well, you're the very one for the job. He must be so concerned with the air pollution in Beijing. But a lot of people here are complaining about it too.'

'Yes, he is concerned,' he said, not eager to dwell on the topic. 'Incidentally, I have to thank you for those assignments you gave me all those years ago – to show the visiting foreign writers around the city, so the current job for Comrade Secretary Zhao may not be too difficult for me.'

It was true. In the days when Chen had first become a member of the Writers' Association, being the only writer capable of speaking English at the time, he was frequently chosen by Qiang as a representative to meet with Western writers, which meant good opportunities for Chen to practice English with them and to enjoy the government-sponsored lavish banquets in honor of them too. He was grateful to Qiang for these arrangements, and Qiang also came to trust Chen. At one point, Qiang had suggested that Chen should succeed him at the office after his retirement, representing Chen as a perfect candidate. With Chen's rise in the police bureau, however, the idea was dropped.

With those memories flashing back, Chen pulled out the white plastic gift bag from the train.

'Here's something I bought on the train. Some Wuxi specials.

Nothing but a token of my gratitude to your help for all these years.'

'Thank you, Chief Inspector Chen. So you've been to Wuxi again,' Qiang said. 'It's so kind of you to think of a retiring old man like me.'

It was a decision made on the spur of the moment. But those Wuxi products were what he had intended for his mother. Later, he had to buy something else for her.

'I've just been too busy, you know. You told me you're going to live with your son in Hangzhou. Like in a proverb: high up there, there's the heaven, and down here, there're Suzhou and Hangzhou. That's surely wonderful, but—'

'But we won't be able to see each other like before—'

'Director Qiang,' a woman in her early thirties burst into the office with a folder in her hand. 'Sorry, I did not know you had a guest. Here is a printout for the office schedule for the week.'

'Chief Inspector Chen of the Shanghai Police Bureau is no guest here, Meiling.'

'Yes, Chief Inspector Chen, I've just recognized you,' the office assistant named Meiling said, smiling before turning to Qiang. 'Take your time reading it.'

As Meiling stepped out of the office, Qiang too stood up and said, 'You have brought me these specials all the way from Wuxi, so I have to accept them. But let me buy you a cup of tea downstairs, that's the least I can do.'

The association had recently had one section of its red brick wall pulled down, in which place an elegant-looking café was built. The café enjoyed good business because of its locale, brought in some extra income for the association, and also made it convenient for the editors to receive their visitors there.

But it was not a day for Chen to talk long with Qiang for old times' sake. The inspector looked hesitant.

'Just for a cup of tea, Chief Inspector Chen. It won't take you much time.'

With Qiang leading the way, the two of them headed into the café.

The young waiter at the door knew both of them, took them

to a corner table looking out to the street, and placed a pot of tea between them.

'It's an important gesture for Comrade Secretary Zhao to have you as his tourist guide in Shanghai,' Qiang said, breathing slowly into the fresh-brewed tea. 'A symbolic gesture of his trust in you from the Forbidden City.'

'I'm just trying to do my job here in Shanghai. A lot of things in Beijing are totally beyond me.'

'You don't have to say that.' Qiang paused before changing the subject. 'I'm going to retire. Nothing really matters that much for me any more, but you still have a long way to go. It won't hurt to be careful.'

That sounded like a signal. Inspector Chen immediately put himself on high alert.

'In addition to your long poem about Tai Lake, you've recently published an article about judicial independence, haven't you?'

'Yes?'

'People came to the foreign liaison office about it.'

'They're interested in my writing?'

'You're a talented writer, everybody knows, but some could be just curious, asking all sorts of questions, about the article, about your working here for the association, your meeting and talking with Western writers here.'

'When did they come to you with these questions?'

'Several months ago.'

'But I've been so busy of late. The last time I met with any visiting Western writers in the association here was more than half a year ago. So they may have been disappointed.'

'Exactly. I told them little they might be interested in. They mentioned your modernist poems, of course, and I said I'm no literary critic. I also said you're not only a productive writer, but also an exemplary Party-member cadre, doing all the volunteer work for the association.'

'Thank you so much, Director Qiang!'

By now, he knew for sure Qiang did not want him down here simply for a cup of tea, though the old man kept talking in a roundabout way.

'Somebody even mentioned an American woman cop who

once worked with you here in Shanghai, but that had nothing to do with those activities at the association. You're such a celebrity, Chief Inspector Chen, people cannot help being so curious about you.'

'There's an English proverb: curiosity killed the cat,' Chen said, without knowing what else to say for the moment. Sometimes old proverbs could turn out to be helpful just because of that.

'It may be just part of their routine work.' Qiang rose and drained the cup of tea, then added, 'For the future promotion in store for you, you may have to go through the process under the Party Central Discipline Committee.'

'I don't know anything about that.'

Chen took it as a far-fetched interpretation, or a cover for the hidden message.

'But I know you're busy, especially with Comrade Secretary Zhao in Shanghai, so I'd better not take up too much of your time. Again, thank you so much, Chief Inspector Chen.'

'Thank you, Qiang. Let me know the date when there's a retirement party for you at the association.'

'I will, bye.'

Peiqin found herself stepping into the *Wenhui* building on the corner of Shanxi and Weihai Roads.

It was a decision made earlier in her restaurant office, after searching for the latest posts about Xiang and Geng with little success. Not only were the posts with the video in the background blocked, but also the posts just mentioning the names of Xiang and Geng.

The net cops had done a thorough job. The several VPN apps she had used also broke down that morning. No possibility of her climbing over the walls, in spite of what she had told Yu the previous night.

It then occurred to her that she might as well do something different. Something Chen had hinted for her to do.

A visit to Lianping at *Wenhui Daily*.

She had first met Lianping in a Buddhist service at Longhua Temple, to which Chen had unexpectedly brought her along. At the time, Peiqin had thought the bachelor inspector was finally ready to settle down in the company of the young journalist, but to Peiqin's disappointment, Lianping shortly afterward married another young man from a rich family. Like in an old Chinese saying, for a man lucky in his official career, he has to be unlucky in romantic affairs. In fact, Chen was said to have had two 'girlfriends' in the newspaper, but was simply luckless both times.

She did not know how things really stood between Chen and Lianping, but not too long ago Lianping had proved that she was still more than willing to help as far as Chen was concerned.

At the entrance of the *Wenhui* building, a doorman stopped Peiqin and demanded registration with her ID. Besides the ID, she had to call the person she wanted to visit.

As luck would have it, Lianping was in the office that morning and picked up the phone at the first ring.

'It's me, Peiqin. The Dragon Boat Festival is coming around. At the restaurant, we have some special *Zongzi* with pork and salted yolk stuffing. So I'm bringing some over to you.'

'It's so kind of you, Peiqin. *Zongzi* with pork and salted yolk stuffing is really popular this year. I've seen long lines of customers circling the Apricot Blossom Pavilion. I'll be coming down in a minute.'

In about five minutes, Lianping hurried out of the elevator with a bulging black purse in her hand.

'Wow, such a large basket, Peiqin. How can I ever thank you enough? It's the least I can do to take you to the café on the street corner. My office upstairs is such a mess.'

Leaving the basket of *Zongzi* on the doorman's table, she took Peiqin's hand like an old friend.

With her stomach slightly rounded in early pregnancy, Lianping still appeared to be young and agile, leading the way to the café in light steps.

'What favorable wind has brought you here – apart from the delicious *Zongzi*?' Lianping said as soon as she seated herself opposite Peiqin at a table by the window. 'Something I can do for you today?'

She tried not to immediately bring Chen into the talk, which Peiqin understood.

'Well, like in a proverb, people do not go to the temple without praying for something. It's about one of the victims in a case investigated by my husband, Yu. She's from your newspaper.'

'That's what I've guessed. About Xiang, right? In fact, this café is not far from the crime scene.' After taking a small sip at the coffee, Lianping added, 'What do you want to know?'

'To be honest, I have no idea what Yu exactly wants to know for the investigation, but how about telling me what you know about her?'

'Then let's go from the beginning. Xiang came to the newspaper about a year ago in an unusual way. A *Wenhui* job is generally considered a very good one. Secure, excellent pay, not to mention the benefits for a journalist in the age of connections. It's difficult even for an MA graduate to land a job here. Xiang's from Anhui Province, and having graduated from a two-year program in a third-class college she had no proper training or qualification whatsoever in the field.

'People naturally had stories about the circumstances of her getting the job. Without going into details for the moment, suffice it to say that she obtained it because of her husband, Geng Hua, the head of Wenxin Group. In the crony socialism of China, such an arrangement was not a surprise. If anything is surprising at all, it is that Xiang did not choose to be a housewife – an enviable status in today's society.

'To be fair to her, Xiang had been working hard here without throwing up any air like a young, spoiled wife of a high-ranking Party official might do. On the contrary, she kept her tail tucked in, so to speak.

'It took just a couple of months for her to become the head of the new economy section, though there're people who've worked here much longer. Having said that, it's not an easy job for her. As a rule, the section head had to work late twice a week, as the newspaper gave half a page to the section Wednesday and Friday. The final galley had to be signed by the person in charge before it's sent to print early in the morning. It was said that our editor in chief told her that she did not have to do so, considering her responsibility to take care of Geng, but she insisted on doing it most of the time. Last

Thursday, with her husband away in Beijing for a meeting, she came to the office for the night shift.

'On that fatal Friday morning, with all the contents of the section proofread and set up, it was around five thirty. She hurried out alone under a gray sky for her favorite Shanghai morning snack – earthen oven cake with fried dough stick from a stall around the street corner.

'Usually, she would come back to the office in five to ten minutes. There's nothing on the street for her to see so early in the morning.

'But she did not come back as usual. No one in the office paid attention to it at first. With the job done, she could have gone wherever she pleased. About an hour later, however, a police officer hurried into the *Wenhui* building.

'Her body was discovered on the street corner still wearing the *Wenhui* name tag over her white silk blouse. She appeared to have suffered a fatal blow from behind with a heavy, blunt object.

'According to the police report, there were some things puzzling about the crime. It's not exactly one of the central locations of the city, with just a few people moving around there in the early hours. For instance, there are only those working for the newspapers, and some customers going to that popular snack stall as soon as it starts business around five fifteen. Why should the criminal have chosen to attack there and then?'

'What a story! I'll tell all this to Yu,' Peiqin said, taking a sip of the cooling coffee, which she did not like. 'Now, have you heard of anything specific about her experience before her coming to work here?'

'Gossip about her, and about him, had been around before her arrival here. Particularly about where she had worked – as a massage girl in a private club,' Lianping said, stirring the spoon slowly in the cup. 'Again, it's not something too surprising. According to a colleague of mine in the entertainment section, quite a number of young college graduates choose to work in those dubious "clubs" or "massage salons". Excellent pay for them. That background, and their college education as extra qualification, is sometimes a must to the

Big Bucks who can show them off not just with their voluptuous bodies, but with their intelligent talk too. For a young
girl like Xiang from Anhui Province, anxious to stay on in
Shanghai, her working at such a temporary job was
understandable.'

'But people all know what the job there is really about?'

'You bet! The moment the massage room door is closed,
what's happening inside is pretty much imaginable,' Lianping
said, producing a laptop and inserting a flash memory card
into it. 'You have not seen the video tape, have you?'

'No, I haven't. Nor has Yu.'

'No need to play it here. Perhaps one image from the tape
may tell you more than enough.'

Sure enough, it vividly demonstrated what was happening
inside the massage room. Geng was sitting on the massage
bed with his pants pulled down to his ankles, and with her
nestling stark naked, leaning partially on his lap and partially
on the edge of the massage bed, one of her long legs stretching
out, her bare foot pressing the door, making sure it was closed.
The old man was forcefully rubbing her hairy crotch to a
climax, her eyes closed in ecstasy.

It was like a graphic movie scene.

'Judging by the date printed on the video, it was about one
month before he married her.'

'Who could have taken the video?'

'I don't know. But the scene is unmistakable. You see, the
door is not supposed to be locked, though no one there will
ever bump in. To make sure of it, she's stretching her foot
hard against the door. That detail explains everything.'

'Yes, everything.'

'You can have the copy for your husband if he does not
have one yet.'

'That will really help, thank you so much.' She added with
a smile, 'He may want me to bring more *Zongzi* to you in the
future.'

'That will be great, but you don't have to come with *Zongzi*.
Anything else I can do to help?'

'About that morning, you have some more details?'

'I work in the literature and art section, and I've learned

things from Zhou, who's also in Xiang's section. In fact, Zhou showed her the ropes in the office when she first came here. I can ask around, and I'll let you know when I get anything new.' Lianping added casually, 'By the way, what's Chief Inspector Chen's take?'

So finally she's coming round to him. But Peiqin did not think she knew enough to say much. Either about the case or about what Lianping really wanted to know.

'He's just got another assignment from Beijing. From someone at the top. Busy as always. He's not on the case we are talking about.'

'He's so busy – always restless.'

'Restless, you can say that again. It's infectious, now to my husband, too. Yu is becoming more and more like his partner. I cannot but be concerned.'

'Your husband is a much more down-to-earth kind, Inspector Chen told me. He's a very high opinion of Detective Yu. You don't have to worry about it.'

After draining the tea in one gulp, Inspector Chen walked out of the café.

For an experienced, cautious old Party cadre like Qiang, it must have been a calculated move, Chen reflected, to take him down for a cup of tea at the café instead of in the office. It was because of a warning Qiang had to give, which the inspector had to take in earnest.

He had no idea, however, what he could do about it, and he decided not to worry too much for the moment.

There were a number of small, exotic cafés scattered along Julu Road. Half a block to the west he saw one with a large poster of Old Shanghai on the door; several more had period decorations on the wall. There was no customer sitting at a table outside.

He stepped in. No customer inside either. He took a seat with a view of the street.

A waitress put a cup of coffee on the table for him and withdrew into a back room. So he had the café for himself.

Sipping at a cup of coffee, he took out his cellphone to call some of his Big Buck associates.

It was another long shot. For a large city like Shanghai, the people he knew would not likely turn out to be the people Shanshan knew.

Still, it wouldn't hurt to give it a try. Some of them might have heard of her or the activist group.

The first two or three phone calls did not yield any result, which he expected. The next one on the calling list was Mr Gu, the chairman of the New World Group, who picked up the phone at the first ring.

'What a coincidence! I was thinking of calling you too, my dear Chief Inspector Chen.'

'What's up, Mr Gu?'

'I'm just leaving the American Consulate with my wife and daughter—'

'Are you emigrating, too?'

'Not me, but my family. I'm accompanying them for the visa interview, but there's still a long line waiting at this moment. I don't think we'll have any luck today. By the way, you know someone in the Consulate, don't you?'

'Well, the Culture Consul has invited me to some literature events at the Consulate. Because of my translation of the American poems, I think. But what do you want me to do for you – to help reduce the line, so to speak, through my connection?'

'Yes, if that's possible, Chief Inspector Chen.'

'I may be able to have a try, but I wonder whether the American would give me the Chinese face, if you know what I mean. Theirs is not exactly a culture of connections.'

'Connections work everywhere in the world. East or West. We're now living in the global age.'

'But you're so successful in your business, with the New World, and with all other real estate properties in China, Mr Gu. Why do you want your family to leave in a hurry?'

'Successful I may be here today, but who can tell what will happen tomorrow? The Party policies change every year. Last year we were encouraged to invest out of China, but this year, with the slowing economy, we're accused of moving our assets abroad. The Party is capable of changing the law and taking things back from you any time it pleases.'

'But you don't have to worry about it right now, Mr Gu.'

'But I have to worry for my family when something is happening in front of my eyes right here. You have heard of the air quality monitor at the American Embassy, haven't you? What an irony! Of late, it has surely become one of the main reasons why so many Chinese people are anxious to apply for American visas.'

'Come on, Mr Gu. You don't have to go there to take a look at the monitor . . .' He did not finish the sentence as he recalled the *Weibo* post he had read the day before. 'Yes, I now remember something about the American air quality monitor incident. What a shame! I did not follow it too closely.'

'You were just too busy with one high-priority investigation after another. But back to the monitor: however the government spokesman tried to deny the fact of China's air pollution as recorded in it,' Mr Gu went on emphatically, as if in an earnest attempt to defend the emigration decision for his family, 'information available in the global age eventually compelled the Beijing authorities to include the PM 2.5 in the air quality index in recognition of the problem.'

'Yes, the government spokesman then justified the inclusion as the progress of national environmental awareness, I read that part too.'

'Progress or not, for the last several days, each and every hospital in the city has been full of patients suffering from respiratory problems. Especially young children. A considerable number of people want to emigrate because of it. You may not believe it but one of my daughter's schoolmates was recently diagnosed with leukemia. Imagine it happening to a boy at such a young age.'

'Yes, people want to go abroad because of the polluted air. But in the meantime, something should be done here about it. In fact, I've just heard that a group of activists are involved in such a project and several of them being Big Bucks too, possibly even in your circle.'

'Oh that . . .' Gu was silent for a moment before going on. 'People ought to do something about the environmental crisis here, no question about it, but I don't know any of those activists, not personally.'

'You're just too busy expanding your business, General Manager Gu.'

'Now we've had our exchange of compliments, Chief Inspector Chen. But I'm not saying that others may not know any of the activists. You've been to the Oriental Club in the New World, haven't you?'

'Yes?'

'One of the club members named Bian has talked to me about the air problem quite a few times. I'm not sure if he is an activist, but he's an air purifier manufacturer with possible connections to the experts and activists in the field. I'll text you his phone number. When you call, you may mention my name. I believe he will answer your questions.'

'Thank you so much, Mr Gu. You're so well connected. I know I can count on you.'

'It's an honor for you to think of me. You know what? Some people are describing you as one of the few honest cops left – like an endangered species . . . or like the public phone booths left on the Shanghai streets.' He then added, as though in afterthought, 'There'll be a movie event at the Consulate next week. If I'm going there, I'll see what I can do.'

A couple of minutes after the phone conversation, a text message came in presenting Bian's phone number, which Chen immediately dialed.

'My name is Chen Cao, of the Shanghai Police Bureau. Your friend Mr Gu, Chairman of the New World Group, has just given me your number suggesting I contact you. I would like very much to have a talk with you.'

'I've heard of you, Chief Inspector Chen. Mr Gu's spoken so highly of you. I have a business appointment this evening, how about meeting for afternoon tea in the Glamorous Bar in an hour?' Bian agreed readily on the phone.

As a consultant to the murder investigation, it was perhaps all Detective Yu could do, he thought gloomily, to make a close study of the evidence – particularly the pictures from the crime scenes, in addition to the material in the case folder from Qin, which Yu had already read a couple of times.

In the evidence room, he was also able to view the videos and pictures gathered from the surveillance cameras at those locations. Some of the pictures were just sent in; he wondered whether Detective Qin had studied them yet.

Qin must have been having another meeting with Internal Security.

After printing out a large number of the pictures, Yu remained sitting alone, spreading them out into four groups along the desk. It was easier to study them like that.

At least one of the points discussed between Yu and Qin was proven. Nothing from any of the surveillance cameras showed the possible suspect.

Among the dramatic changes in the city in the last several years, one was the installation of an incredibly large number of surveillance cameras, practically everywhere, and particularly in those central locations. It was done, like a lot of things, in the name of 'stability maintenance'. In the age of the increasingly popular social media sites like *Weixin* or *Weibo*, the government was worried about sudden eruptions of people's protests.

So it meant, among other things, that the murderer must have done a reconnaissance trip beforehand.

Perhaps he was not only young or middle-aged, but also an agile, alert man who knew something about the surveillance technologies.

Like Qin, Yu was not that sure about Chen's theory. Whatever coup Chen had produced with the previous serial murder, this was a different case, with nothing like a red mandarin dress as a possible lead.

Under the light of the evidence room, Yu spent quite a period of time going over the pictures one by one, regrouping them from a variety of angles, enlarging them on the computer screens, and reprinting some.

Then he thought they had another thing in common. In the four groups of the crime scene pictures, each showed the presence of a mask.

Of the four, victim number two was wearing a mask on his face, but not the other three. Two of those had masks that had dropped to the ground, close to their bodies, possibly due to the violent strikes they'd suffered; but for number three, it was actually at a distance from her body. At first, Yu did not even notice it as a mask. It was visible only in one picture in the group; in the enhanced resolution it showed a slight yellowish color, looking like a lost handkerchief.

It was perhaps nothing that uncommon, however, for people to wear masks for these smoggy mornings.

Still, it left a question mark in Detective Yu's mind.

Glamorous Bar was one of the top fancy restaurants in Shanghai, located on the corner of the Bund and Guangdong Road. The seventh-floor balcony boasted a superb view of Pudong, the east side of the river. It was said that a large number of customers went there for the view.

But Chen and Bian turned out to be the only customers sitting on the balcony that day. Like the day before, the view appeared shrouded in an impenetrable grayness.

Bian was in his mid- or late-forties with a balding headline and constantly blinking eyes. Taking a cigarette from him without lighting it, Chen realized he should have made a more serious effort to quit smoking. Like so many in the city, he suffered from a sore throat, a symptom increasingly common, even among the people who did not smoke.

A blonde waitress came over, stepping light-footed as if floating out of the enveloping smog, moving to their table with a silver tray that contained a dainty coffee set, a fruit-topped white cake and a well-printed menu.

'The Pavlova cake here is the best in the city,' Bian said, stirring the coffee cup. 'I cannot resist the sight of Pavlova in spite of my relatively high blood sugar. Melody knows that only too well about me.'

Apparently a regular customer here, Bian nodded at the waitress named Melody, who left the tray on their table, smiling an engaging smile before she disappeared back into the murkiness.

'So you are associated with Yuan Jing – or Shanshan as I used to call her in Wuxi,' Chen said as soon as the waitress left them alone, taking the direct approach.

'Shanshan – ah, you must know her well. Yes, she's such

a celebrity; a lot of people know her in Shanghai or elsewhere.'

'I met with her in Wuxi, but that was several years ago. So can you tell me something about her now – about the environmental project you are working on with her?'

'I've heard a lot about you, Chief Inspector Chen. Mr Gu spared no effort recommending you as a trustworthy and reliable one,' Bian responded deliberately, looking him in the eye. 'Still, can you tell me first why you suddenly want to find out things about the project in relation to her?'

'A leading comrade from Beijing wants me to look into it, that much I can tell you, though I do not know his real purpose either,' Chen said, producing a copy of *Shanghai Literature* and turning to the page with the poem on it. 'But let me show you a poem first.'

'"Don't Cry, Tai Lake." So you wrote it? Yes, you're also a poet.' Bian took the magazine and started reading in undisguised astonishment. 'Sorry, I did not know anything about it.'

'That's little wonder. You can hardly find any literature magazines at newsstands in the city.'

'For that matter, hardly any newsstands still in existence in the true sense of the word,' Bian said with an annoyed wave of his hand. 'There used to be one not far from the corner of Guangdong and Sichuan Roads, just a stone's throw from here, but it now sells chestnuts and other dry nuts instead.'

With Bian still reading the poem, Chen took a sip of the coffee and looked up across the river, east of which surely appeared 'the financial center of Asia'. An almost surreal forest of modern or ultramodern high-rises loomed through a smoggy mirage; Pudong certainly appeared more magnificent than Puxi, Zhao was right about that, which had been developed much earlier during the days of the British concession.

It began drizzling, just a little, but they were sitting under the awning.

'A great poem, Chief Inspector Chen,' Bian said, without looking up from the page. 'I wonder how you could have produced it. In the company of Yuan – oh, Shanshan, right?'

The chief inspector nodded without making an instant response.

Yes, it was in Wuxi, in the bedroom of a luxurious suite in the Cadre Recreation Center . . .

Afterward, it started to rain. He listened to it pattering against the windows as he sat up, placing the laptop on his drawn-up knees, imagining the lake furling around like a girdle in a poem he remembered.

To his surprise, she flung one arm over, her fingers brushing against the keyboard before grasping his leg, as if anxious to reassure herself of his still being beside her in sleep. An accidental touch that brought up some of the lines he had composed earlier by the lake.

Then he began working with a multitude of images surging up, thinking of the lone, hard battle she had been fighting for the lake.

> Soon, the spring is departing again.
> How much more of wind and rain
> can it really endure? Only the cobweb
> still cares, trying to catch
> a touch of the fading memory.
> Why is the door always covered
> in the dust of doubts?
> The lake cries, staring
> at the silent splendid sun.
> Who is the one walking beside you?

The lines were still disorganized, but it was imperative for him to put all of them down there without a break. He went on typing, juxtaposing one scene with another, jumping among the stanzas, worrying little about the structure or the syntax for the moment.

Realities, too, were disorganized.

He tried to visualize the hardships she had been going through, working against the odds at her environmental protection job, alone, day after day.

But what had he done? As a successful Party member cop enjoying all the privileges, and now even as a 'high-ranking cadre' at the center, he had paid little attention to the

*environmental issue. He was simply too busy being Chief
Inspector Chen, someone rising in the system.*

*Pushing a strand of sweat-matted hair from her forehead,
he wished he had met her earlier, and learned more about her
work, albeit beyond his field. He was going to introduce an
intimate touch to the next stanza, imagining a talk with her
about the lake . . .*

Finally, Bian was reaching the end of the long poem, forking
up the last bit of Pavlova cake from the plate with a sigh of
contented regret, when Inspector Chen turned his gaze back
from afar and said to him in earnest, 'To tell the truth, it was
Shanshan that inspired me for the poem by the lake. But that's
something I have not told the magazine editor. Nor the leading
comrade from Beijing, as you may understand.'

'Really!'

'Make no mistake about it, Bian. It was quite a few years
ago that I met her on a vacation in Wuxi. I've since not seen
or heard from her. That's why anything you tell me about her
may prove to be so helpful.'

'Thank you so much for your trust in me, Chief Inspector
Chen.'

'You don't have to thank me for anything. But this I do
want you to know, Bian: whatever environmental project
Shanshan may be engaged in, I will do whatever possible to
keep any harm from happening to her. I give you my word
about it.'

'I'm so glad you tell me all that, Chief Inspector Chen. The
air pollution is such a national disaster, I don't think I need to
go over that with you in detail, but not all Chinese people can
afford to go abroad for fresh air, not like Mr Gu's family. For
them, masks and air purifiers may prove to be the only help
available. The air purifiers manufactured by my company sell
at the average price of seven or eight thousand yuan per unit,
with some premium brands for more than fifteen thousand.
Believe it or not, they all keep selling like hot cakes.'

'Wow, it's more than the monthly pay for an ordinary worker
in the city.'

'Do you think people have any choice? The lung cancer

rate for the country is increasing so rapidly. The authorities will never attribute it to the contaminated air, but even the government spokesman cannot totally deny it.'

'Yes, I've read about it too,' Chen said, nodding. 'According to the government-run *China Daily*, China has more lung-cancer diagnoses and fatalities than any other country in the world, with over 600,000 dying of the disease every year at the present.'

'So you see, it's the same deadly air people are all breathing. How can they afford not to be worried? Some wealthy parents at my son's school wanted to install an air purifier in the classroom at their own expense. But the district authorities vetoed the idea, saying such a precedent could not be set, which would harm the image of the city. It's such a crying shame for me to make tons of money out of the crisis, as my wife keeps harping on at me.'

'It's just part and parcel of the market economy, you cannot do anything about it, Bian. No need to be so hard on yourself. But how did you move from the fresh air machine to Shanshan's project?'

'Again, it's because of my wife, a newly converted Buddhist believer suffering from asthma. So appalled at the idea of "cashing in on people's miseries", she insisted that I should do something about the terrible air quality. Redemption, you know, in accordance with the Buddhist scripture she reads every day. Then I happened to hear about Shanshan.'

'I see, so you went out of your way to help her project.'

'With the severe smog, and with the Party's continuous emphasis on GDP, I don't think an activist like Shanshan alone can make a real difference anytime soon. Not in ten or fifteen years, I'm afraid. Besides, it does not cost that much to help with her environmental documentary—'

'Hold on, Bian. Shanshan is making a documentary?'

'Yes, it's a research documentary about the air pollution in China.'

'But how could it be possible for such a movie to come out under the government censorship?'

'Censorship is a matter of course in the socialism of China's characteristics – that is if the documentary is ever going to make its way into the movie theater. But for something put on the Internet, with a stroke of luck, it could be a different story.'

'That's intriguing, Bian.'

'Theoretically, it's permissible for people to post a video online as long as there's no anti-government stuff in it. With those latest smartphones, they can so easily make videos for fun – a clip of several minutes or a bit longer, no big deal like before. The government is not too worried about it. After all, it can be instantly blocked once the net cops find in it anything politically incorrect or dangerous.'

'But how long is her research documentary?'

'Longer than one hour, I think, covering a considerable number of aspects. Possibly an hour and a half.'

'So it's quite professionally made – not at all like those cellphone video clips?'

'Yes, as professionally as you can imagine.'

'But what about the funding for the production of such a professionally made documentary?'

'That's where we came in, offering to cover a part of the expense,' Bian said with a touch of pride. 'Several other entrepreneurs like me. At the end of the movie, Shanshan will make a list of donors for the project. To be honest, that shall be a marvelous marketing opportunity for our companies. Exceptional PR work. Really worth every penny we have put in.'

'Is she that well known?'

'Quite well known, I should say, especially in our circle. And among the netizens too, who follow her posts all the time. But of course, you don't say a single word about the documentary to others, not even to that leading comrade from Beijing. Not until after its release.'

'Not a single word, you don't have to worry about it. I totally understand, Bian.'

For a privately funded documentary about the national environmental crisis, Chen observed, its eventual release to a large audience appeared to be open to question, when the net cops kept prowling around. So the secrecy of its production could be crucial, as Bian emphasized.

But how was it possible that people like Zhao – and Internal

Security too – had not heard something about it? It was a puzzle, to which he had no answer.

'So the documentary will be put on one particular website?'

'Well, more than one. You know how much those websites depend on commercials?' Bian said with a proud smile. 'My company put a lot of them on the New Waves website. Its owner knows what a favor he owes me for them, and he promised he would have the documentary on as soon as it's available.'

'But it can be a huge risk to him – and the website, too.'

'Well, it's a calculated risk. The website people can claim that they know nothing about its contents, and it's simply put on there by somebody unknown to them. So it may not necessarily spell too much trouble. Besides, it's not just me alone doing that. My associates are taking care of the remaining major websites. When the documentary appears simultaneously on each and every major website, plus the instant forwarding and reposting among the netizens all over the country, it will be such a national hit, the government may have a really hard time dealing with it.'

'I see. Like in an old Chinese saying: the law may not be able to punish too many people. Still, it's so generous of you to do so.'

'It's no waste of money as far as my product line goes. The commercials have to appear somewhere anyway. Why not for the movie? Imagine my company name shown at the end of it – to be seen by millions and millions.'

'Are you also involved in the process of the documentary making?'

'No, not exactly. Shanshan has a free hand with the production, but she sees to the effective communication and discussion among all of us. We are encouraged to express our opinions about it. For instance, some of us want to make sure that the film does not go too far, lest it might not be able to come out, or even if it did, it would get instantly banned. Then it would amount to a waste of effort and money. Needless to say, none of us wants to get ourselves into serious troubles with the government. We have to do business in the system.'

'Yes, all of us have to walk a tightrope in the system.'

'You can say that again, Chief Inspector Chen.' Bian added after a short pause, 'In fact, there will be a meeting at the Oriental Club tomorrow afternoon. It's in the New World, you know.'

'Oriental Club, I know. So it's tomorrow afternoon – are you going there, Bian?'

'We don't have to attend each and every one of those meetings. Occasionally, we send our representatives there. So we'll have some ideas about how things are moving along.'

'How about,' Chen said, draining the cold coffee in one gulp, 'sending me there as your representative tomorrow? I'll simply sit there and listen without saying a word, that much I can promise you. No one will pay any attention to me.'

'I think that may work, but I just want to say it once again: it's a good, much-needed project, that documentary about the air pollution in China.'

'I cannot agree more,' Chen said emphatically. 'Let me give you my word again: no harm will happen to her, or to the documentary.'

Detective Yu was still poring over the pictures when his special phone rang.

'We have added the noodles stirred with fried green onion oil and dried shrimp to the list of the Shanghai Number One Noodles,' Peiqin said on the phone. 'You have to come. So delicious, you would bite your tongue off.'

'Shanghai Number One Noodles . . .' That was the joke between Inspector Chen and Peiqin. She would not have called into his new phone about it, whether a chef's special had been added to the list or not. 'But I'm in the middle of something here. Bring it home tonight.'

'You won't regret it for your trip. Lianping too likes it so much.'

'Lianping?'

'She also brought me a new video. A very exciting one.'

'Very well then, I'm on my way.'

Now Detective Yu knew why Peiqin called.

*　　*　　*

When Inspector Chen finally got back to his apartment he collapsed into the chair close to the computer, too drained to reach out to click the mouse.

It might not have been such an eventful day for him as a cop – he had had worse ones – but there was still a lot for him to do before he could call it a day, and a lot for him to worry about in terms of what might come the next day.

But in the midst of all these wandering thoughts, he took out the pictures from Huang and dismissed the fear of whatever might happen next.

He began to spread them out one by one on the table, like at the Wuxi hotel room in the morning.

Then one picture seemed to be jumping out to him, which showed her lying on her back with her crossed arms covering her bare breasts, nestling against Yao who was holding up her bare foot, caressing the red-painted toes like petals . . .

It was far from a pleasant experience for him to go through those pictures of Shanshan lying beside another man.

The dusk was quickly sinking into darkness, as if on the wings of an ominous black bird.

There's no blaming Shanshan for her earlier decision to not leave Jiang for him, Chen told himself. She did not know Jiang's marital status at the time. Nor for her subsequent decision to leave Jiang for Yao in the changed circumstances.

The inspector had stayed far away, long out of touch, too busy with his own work in the system.

Since their parting in Wuxi, he had tried only once to contact her – to have the magazine office send her a copy of *Shanghai Literature* with the poem in it – without giving away his own mailing address.

Was it done out of magnanimity, as Huang called it? No, he did not think so. It was nothing but a pathetic pose dictated by the wounded ego.

Under the lamplight, Shanshan looked slightly tanned in those pictures. In one of them, she was stretching out gracefully on the beach, showing sand stuck on her feet and toes. Again, there was something strangely familiar, reminiscent of her stepping out barefoot from the sampan to the lake shore.

It was not a night for him to indulge in romantic nostalgia, he knew, but he succumbed to the temptation of pulling out the magazine again, and came upon the ending of 'Don't Cry, Tai Lake'.

> *Who is the one walking beside you?*
> *By the water, an apple tree*
> *blossoming again, flashing*
> *smiles among the waking boughs,*
> *petals transparent in the dazzling light,*
> *she walks in a red trench coat*
> *carries a report in her hand*
> *like a bright sail cutting*
> *through the contaminated currents*
> *to the silent splendid sun.*

It was an optimistic ending, suggested by the editor for the sake of circumventing government censorship, which Chen understood and complied.

But it was also a scene he had been envisioning, in a sentimental fantasy, time and again.

In a fleeting figment of imagination, she seemed to be coming over to him just like that, with the white apple blossom dazzling under the sun, her arms reaching out, smiling after the successful release of the documentary, and inhaling the new fresh air.

But what about the development in real life – in his as well as hers?

> *Willows at Zhangtai, willows at Zhangtai,*
> *still so green as in the past?*
> *The soft, long shoots still clinging –*
> *in another man's hand . . .*

The lines from the Tang dynasty poem came back to him like a satirical echo of the present moment, of the poem he was holding in his hand.

The refrain '*Who is the one walking beside you?*' had been originally put in there as a means for the spatial structure of his poem, but in his subconscious mind he must have projected himself into the 'one', and not just in the lines of the poem.

Now the refrain read like a self-fulfilled sign. It's somebody else, not him, walking beside her at the moment.

And he was doing the investigation as a cop, not as a poet, with the utmost detachment imaginable for him.

As if through a mysterious correspondence in cyberspace, Detective Yu gave Inspector Chen an unexpected call.

'You know where Old Hunter will be in the morning, Chief?'

'The Bird Corner in People's Park. It's good for your father to really enjoy his life in retirement in the midst of twittering birds.'

'Tomorrow morning, he wants to show you a new bird he has just got. A very sexy bird.'

'Really!'

He had met Old Hunter there before – not for the sake of birds.

Nor could it be the real reason for the meeting next morning. It would probably be something not safe for Detective Yu to send electronically.

'I'll be there. Six o'clock. I've not seen him for a couple of months.'

Chen thought he got the hint about the 'sexy bird'. And he also had to get a new email address for himself.

DAY THREE
WEDNESDAY

Early Wednesday morning, Detective Yu went to have another talk with Detective Qin in his office.

'You're not our legendary infallible chief inspector, Detective Yu,' Qin started with a tone quite different from the day before, 'so I'll keep nothing from you.'

'Thanks, Detective Qin.'

'I think we have got the one with the real motive for Xiang, victim number four.'

'How?'

'It's in the original direction pursued by Internal Security,' Qin said, tapping on the desk with his forefinger. 'From the very beginning, they suspected that it had been done by someone bearing a really deep grudge against Xiang, or against Geng, or against both of them.'

'So they have discovered such a one?'

'Yes, they have. It may not have been too difficult for them, with all the information about her at their disposal. Her promotion to the section head meant, as you'd expect, the exclusion of other candidates for the position. In her section, there's a journalist surnamed Zhou. Having worked there for longer than a decade, he was known as a capable and experienced worker, too. Prior to her arrival at the newspaper, Zhou was acknowledged, though not that officially, as the acting section head in practical charge for the last two years – just like you, in practical charge of your special case squad—'

'Chief Inspector Chen is a friend of mine. He has just been too busy with so many other things, you know,' Yu said, feeling obliged to say something for Chen.

'Whatever you may want to say about your boss, Xiang was not a friend of Zhou's. Her arrival deprived him of the "acting" status. And a couple of months later, far from as

capable or experienced, she was made the section head, which
totally ruled out the possibility of his promotion. How do you
think Zhou would have reacted?'

'It's not fair, but there're so many things not fair in this
world. Old Hunter entered the bureau earlier than Party
Secretary Li. Li has never done a real case. But so what?
People do not kill simply because of—'

'But Zhou had his reason to hate her, and for that matter,
even to hate the newspaper, right?'

'Yes, it's an enormous humiliation for him to have lost it
to such a young girl.'

'Well, it's more than that. He happened to be the one working
with Xiang that evening.'

'That Thursday evening?' Yu said, recalling things Peiqin
had learned from Lianping the previous night, including the
name of Zhou in the background. 'You mean Zhou worked
together with her during the night shift?'

'He left earlier, but he's the one familiar with her routine
during the night shift, and with what she would do after going
through the galley in the early morning. So you see, it really
made sense for someone to have planned the attack with the
knowledge about her movements that morning.'

'But others in her office might also have known about her
partiality for the Shanghai snack. And it's not something invariable; she could have chosen the newspaper canteen for a
change. Nor could anyone have foretold when exactly she
would go down for the earthen oven cake.'

'With Zhou's familiarity about her routine, he could have
waited for her to come down in the early hours.'

'A long, long wait it could have been, not to mention a lot
of cameras around the area. A lone wolf waiting there would
have been so conspicuous in the early morning.'

'But here's another clue,' Qin responded, raising his voice
a little. 'The video cameras at the *Wenhui* building entrance
and exit happened to be down that night. In case of its being
not an accident, Zhou certainly knew how to handle that as
an insider, and for a reason known to him alone. According
to his testimony, he left the office around twelve, but with the
cameras down, that was not verified. He could have stayed on

somewhere inside the building, in view of Xiang walking out, and followed her out to the stall for the fatal blow. He did not have to wait that long outside, standing or strolling about inconspicuously on the street.'

'But I did not know anything about the camera problem at the *Wenhui* building, Detective Qin.'

'Sorry, we too have just learned it.'

Yu did not think that was true. Qin had been reluctant to work with the Special Case squad, or to share the information with him.

'And another question related to the scenario,' Yu went on after a short pause. 'How could Zhou have possibly obtained the video tape at the club?'

'The earlier relationship between Xiang and Geng was no news to the people in the newspaper. Zhou was certainly in a position to have heard about it.'

'But the video was made in the days when she still worked as a massage girl. Zhou came to know her after she started working as a journalist for *Wenhui*. How could that have been possible?'

'At the time, the video was possibly made against Geng.'

'Zhou had no grudge against Geng, had he? I think we have talked about it. No point going over it again. Even if it were the case, it should have been released at the time, with Geng still married to his former wife, and in the position of the vice mayor. So his affair with such a massage girl would have easily made the *Weixin* headline.'

'I think you have made this point before, Detective Yu.'

'And with her recent death, and his being in hospital, some people reacted to the tragedy not without a touch of sympathy.'

'Yes, possibly less damage. But Geng's known as a ruthless man, having crushed his opponents like ants, so one of them could have chosen to have the video come out in a different light. The combination of her death in a sensational murder and his exposure in a salacious massage scene. That could have called so much more public attention and devastated Geng in an irrecoverable way – at least from the revenger's perspective.'

'But the question remains: how could an ordinary journalist like Zhou have got hold of such a video?'

'Internal Security has looked into that. Some club people secretly made videos like that for selling – for a really high price. It might be used for some secret purpose you may never imagine.'

'Another question for your scenario: what about the other victims? They had done nothing against Zhou. In fact, they might not have known him at all.'

'They were killed to make the murder of Xiang even more sensational,' Qin said, with increasingly visible impatience.

'It's difficult for me to imagine Zhou could have done all that for such a reason.'

'Zhou had another deeper reason, like your Inspector Chen says, "known only to himself". He had been seeing a young woman for several years. With the prospect of his being promoted to the section head, and then possibly the associate editor in chief for the newspaper, things were not bad between the two, but she recently dumped him.'

'What's that to do with the murder?'

'With Xiang serving as his boss, he's seen as one with no future. Xiang's much younger, plus with Geng's power behind her, there's no way for him to move up any more, and that's the way Zhou's girlfriend saw it.'

'So you mean he did all the killings as a sort of prelude for the killing of Xiang? But he could have been caught in one of the earlier murders, then his revenge plan would have been totally finished even before it had started. Zhou would have known better.'

'For a serial murderer, he knows only the logic of his twisted mind. *Twisted mind*, isn't that your Inspector Chen's phrase? His choice of those central locations could have been made out of the same consideration. The more sensation, the more devastating to the Gengs.'

Qin was apparently so deep into the scenario pushed by Internal Security, Yu saw no point arguing any more. It was pointless. With no other leads or clues, Internal Security's scenario could have appeared like a life-saving straw to Qin.

But Yu was far from convinced.

* * *

Back in his apartment after meeting with Old Hunter in People's Park, carrying with him a flash memory stick from the old man who had got it from Peiqin the night before, Inspector Chen did not even have the time to really check into the contents of it before he got a text message from Zhao. It was unexpected from the senior Party leader.

'You are moving in the right direction. Good job, Chief Inspector Chen. Keep at it.'

He wondered at Zhao's comment about 'the right direction'. The trip to Wuxi? Nothing like any breakthrough was reported as far as Zhao's inquiry was concerned. Was it in relation to the mention of the petroleum industry in the earlier message from Chen? It did not take a chief inspector to point a finger at its contribution to the air pollution.

The message was too vague.

Again, Chen felt like walking out for a while. The apartment suddenly felt suffocating as he recalled the fresh air machine in Zhao's hotel suite, as well as all the other types of machine Bian had told him about the day before.

He too should have one installed at home – perhaps at his mother's small room first in that old *shikumen* house. He wondered whether he would have the time to visit her the next day, feeling pretty bad about having given away the Wuxi specials to Qiang.

On the street corner, Chen joined a line of people edging toward a Shanghai snack stall. When his turn came, he bought for himself a sesame-covered sticky rice ball, which the peddler ladled out of the sizzling oil in a large wok.

The sticky rice ball tasted hot, soft, sweet with red bean paste inside, but somehow not as tasty as before. Possibly because of the 'gutter oil', he speculated. So many things turned out to be toxic or unhealthy in today's society. Still nibbling at the golden-colored sticky rice ball, he did not want to worry too much about it for the moment, walking aimlessly and thinking.

Then he noticed the young, slender girl who had stood wearing a large mask in front of him in the line at the snack stall. She was now biting a sesame-covered earthen oven cake in her hand, walking abreast of him. The mask off, she looked strikingly vivacious in spite of the sesame stuck to her lips and cheeks in the gray morning.

Was there something youthful about her, reminiscent of Shanshan?

> *Slender, supple, she's just thirteen,*
> *the tip of a cardamom bud*
> *in the early spring . . .*

Chen found his mind helplessly wandering away into Du Mu's lines in the Tang dynasty.

Peiqin was on the way from the state-run restaurant to the private-run eatery, wiping the beads of sweat from her forehead, when she got a text message from Lianping.

'Some people came to talk to Zhou this morning. Zhou worked with Xiang that evening, but he left the office shortly after, around twelve.'

Apparently, it was not a convenient moment for Lianping to talk on the phone in the office. So Peiqin typed a question in response.

'The people from Yu's bureau?'

'No. Not in police uniform.'

'They have found something about Zhou during that night shift, haven't they?'

'That I don't know. For the night shift, usually it requires only one person in charge to stay there. When things get too busy, two or three may stay on in the office. Zhou worked a couple of extra hours that evening before going back home, leaving her alone there.' Lianping then added, 'At least that's the version Zhou gave us about that night. Nothing has been announced in the newspaper, but Zhou left with those men. He looked ghastly pale according to the doorman who saw them walk out. Not handcuffed, though.'

'Thanks. I'll let Yu know.'

Chen was still reprimanding himself for getting lost in Du Mu's Tang dynasty again when he had a phone call come in from Ouyang.

'Something happened, Inspector Chen.'

'What?'

'Qiang disappeared. Mrs Qiang called into the association in the morning. Qiang is a family man, having never stayed out overnight without calling back home. She had dialed his cellphone numerous times, but it remained turned off. That's strange. Because of the nature of his job, he made a point of keeping his phone on all the time. By this morning she got so frantic that she contacted us. People in the association started calling around, too. However, his cellphone is still shut off.'

'That's really strange. What did his office assistant Meiling say?'

'According to Meiling, Qiang had never mentioned any activities scheduled that afternoon or that night.'

'When was Qiang last seen?'

'Yesterday afternoon, shortly after your visit to him, as Meiling recalled.'

'Well, Qiang and I moved down to the café for tea. It was about one thirty, and after twenty minutes or so, he went back to his office.'

'Yes, Meiling saw him coming back to the office, but then he got a phone call and hurried out. He did not say anything to her about it.'

'He could have left for something urgent.'

'He's retiring. For the last several months Meiling was practically in charge of the office work. There was nothing urgent or important scheduled yesterday. Besides, he would have told her if he had to leave because of something related to the office.'

'That beats me, Ouyang. But don't worry too much. I'll try to come over to the association today. By that time, Qiang might have come back with an explanation.'

But Inspector Chen was truly worried about Qiang turning off his phone.

Could his disappearance have had something to do with his talk with the inspector at the café?

If that were the case, the net could be tightening around the inspector, relentlessly, for something still beyond his knowledge.

He must have been followed. His visit to Qiang's office and then to the café downstairs raised the alarm for some, most likely Internal Security, who kept watching for each and every move he was making.

Because of that, Qiang had received 'the invitation out for a cup of tea'.

'The invitation out for a cup of tea' was a newly coined Chinese expression, meaning that people were detained by Internal Security at an unknown location for questioning – for days, or even longer if the 'tea drinker' in question was believed not to have come out with everything useful. It was not seen as formal police procedure, nor acknowledged or reported in the official media. The invitation was carried out without a warrant or anything like that, and the 'tea drinker', usually scared to death by the 'tea experience', would never talk about it afterward.

For Qiang, the questioning possibly revolved around the contents of his talk with Chen in the café.

But both of them had talked carefully. As far as Qiang was concerned, there was nothing but an old man's concerns about a younger colleague, even though some of his words could have been taken as oblique hints, open to different interpretations. On Chen's part, he had not given away anything involving sensitive information. Still, Internal Security would not have believed it. Consequently, Qiang remained detained until he would start telling them what they wanted to uncover.

For an alternative scenario, Qiang could have known much more about Chen's trouble. In order to make sure of his not leaking anything else to Chen, he was detained. That made sense, however, only if something catastrophic was going to happen to Chen really soon – within a matter of days. Until then, would Qiang have to remain in an unknown location holding his cup of tea?

Then Chen recalled something else that afternoon. The office assistant Meiling came in with a printout to Qiang during their talk, upon which Qiang stopped in the middle of a sentence and suggested that they had tea down in the café instead.

Meiling, the designated successor to Qiang, must have been screened and trained by Internal Security. Qiang was aware of the potential complications, so he wanted to continue the talk somewhere else. It nevertheless stirred up suspicions.

All of these could turn out to be wild speculations on the part of the panic-stricken inspector. Nothing but a coincidence with Qiang's disappearance shortly after their talk. But Chen had a hard time bringing himself to believe in the coincidence.

And it could also point toward a different scenario, an even more sinister set-up threatening to engulf both Shanshan and him, which was not that inconceivable, he realized, with pieces already adding up for a disparate picture of the puzzle.

The piece of Zhao choosing him for this job after having made a study of his poem in connection to the once relationship between him and Shanshan; the piece of Zhao and others opting not to do anything directly about her documentary project; the piece of his having ruffled high feathers with his earlier investigations, and with his articles about judicial independence; the piece of her scantily clothed pictures mysteriously surfacing in a net cop's computer . . .

These pieces, when put together, suggested a devilish trap had been set for him in the investigation of Shanshan's project. Considering the past between the two, it was to be expected that they would come to discuss among themselves some things of which she might not have spoken to others. After all, they found themselves in the same boat, so to speak, once in Tai Lake, and now by Huangpu River. She had no reason not to trust him. So the hitherto unknown information would then be uncovered.

In the midst of all this, the piece of Qiang's disappearance could have been designed to make the devious trap infallible.

But he ended up with only one certainty: whoever had orchestrated the disappearance of Qiang must have done so from a really powerful position.

Detective Yu was increasingly disturbed with Qin's direction of the investigation.

Then a phone call came in from Peiqin. After recounting Lianping's message, she added, 'Lianping could not talk in her office, so she texted me, and I texted back. When we were finished, the plum flower cake for brunch was cold.'

'You are the most extraordinary wife for a cop, as Chen has said.'

It was obvious that Internal Security was moving fast in accordance to their set course of action, and so was Detective Qin, following them.

So what else could Detective Yu do?

As a consultant, he had made himself clear enough to Detective Qin who was the one in charge of the investigation, though they all still thought differently.

Lighting a cigarette, Yu decided to study the case report and pictures just one more time.

The contents of the report were so familiar to him that he put it down after no more than ten minutes. There was no point going over the details he had repeatedly studied.

Studying all the pictures once again, however, revealed a similarity between the masks of the first victim and third victim: both with a slight yellowish color. Some masks, if worn for too long, could have discolored, but the color for the two masks in question appeared to be deeper than that. It was possibly because of the material. With such severe air pollution, some high-end manufacturer could have pre-treated the material for better effect.

Sweating, he compared the four groups more closely.

For the second victim, the mask was definitely white. Also, he was wearing it when his body was discovered.

As for the fourth victim, Yu had just a couple of crime scene pictures from Qin in which the mask appeared to be partially covered by the earthen oven cake, with only its straps visible.

Under closer examination, however, the straps looked slightly yellowish too, though Detective Yu was not absolutely sure about the color.

In Qin's case report, there was about half a sentence mentioning the first victim's mask being a much-used one, off color. That made sense, considering her circumstances as a penny-saving night caregiver, but not so with the third. Nor with the fourth. If Xiang's mask also proved to be yellowish, it would be too much of a coincidence – three out of four.

Rearranging the pictures on the desk, and restudying them in comparison, Yu was thunderstruck by another possibility for the first time: except for the second victim wearing the mask on his face, the masks for the other victims could have been planted by their bodies.

And that would be something too strikingly common among the victims. To use Chen's word, the real 'signature', capable of telling them why the murderer had to commit the murder.

But how, Yu still had no clue.

After going over the pictures for another time, Detective Yu pulled out his phone and dialed Peiqin.

'What's up, Yu?'

'Have you seen people wearing a sort of yellowish mask?'

'Not that I can recall. But for young people a variety of patterns and colors would not be unimaginable. I have seen pinkish and florid ones, almost like colorful scarfs.'

'Let me ask a different question. Is it possible for a mask to get yellowish after being repeatedly worn and washed?'

'In my childhood, I used to wear and wash a mask so many times, so it's usable for more than a year. It could have been a bit discolored – not as white as before – but never yellowish. Nowadays, masks are simply something disposable for young people. They don't bother to wash them. But for your question, the answer is no, a mask won't turn yellowish with wear and tear.'

'So you are sure about it?'

'I'm positive. But for all your questions about masks, I have a question for you too.'

'Yes?'

'For the serial murder case, one of the victims was hit while jogging out in the morning?'

'Yes, the third victim, a young girl named Yan.'

'Did she wear a mask while jogging out on a smoggy morning?'

'That's a good question. Yes, she had a mask with her – to be more exact, the mask had fallen aside on the bank, at some distance from her body.' Yu went on after a short pause, 'And for your question, I have another one. If you were aware of breathing all the toxic air into the lungs while jogging out in the smog, would you have chosen to wear a mask?'

'Not me, I simply would not jog outside these days, but I don't know about others. Some people could be crazy enough for their working-out fix in the morning. At least, I've seen mask-wearing people playing tai chi in People's Park. Still, jogging could be a different story. Running, you'll be hard-breathing or even breathless. Think how much more uncomfortable it would be with the horrible air *and* the suffocating mask.'

'Again, your answer is no?'

'I guess I would say so. But what comes over you, Yu? You're suddenly turning into a mask expert. Is this about your investigation again?'

'I'll tell you more this evening.'

After spending more than an hour doing research for the preview in the afternoon, Inspector Chen concluded that it was impractical to prepare without seeing the documentary first.

So he took out the case report, the pictures and the video Detective Yu had sent him via Old Hunter in the park.

Yu had done a good job gathering so much at a short notice, Chen thought, with hardly any cooperation from Detective Qin.

Particularly so for the video, through which he skimmed, wondering how it could be related to the murder case.

He moved on to an examination of the pictures. With the video he had just seen, he paid more attention to those of Xiang. Not just those at the crime scene, but also some in the newspaper. She looked quite an intellectual in the *Wenhui* office, in sharp contrast to the image in the video in the massage room. Then he took a look at those at the crime scene. She lay face down on the street, with the half-finished cake on the curb beside her.

Gazing at the picture for a couple of seconds, he shook his head. He felt sad, tired, not like a cop, or at least not up to the job of a cop.

Still, he had to make a visit to the Shanghai Writers' Association. He had no choice.

Before lunch, Detective Yu dialed Inspector Chen, who picked up the call instantly.

'Something new from Peiqin's talk with Lianping, Chief.'

Yu briefed Chen on what Lianping had told Peiqin regarding Xiang, Zhou, as well as other relevant information.

Chen listened without interruption.

'It's so nice of Lianping,' he said simply.

'Yes, she's really nice.'

Yu then moved on to a detailed description of the investigation he had done into the yellowish masks.

'Great job,' Chen said, raising his voice. 'It's definitely in the right direction, Detective Yu.'

'So you also think it's the signature, just like the torn mandarin dress in the other serial murder case. The criminal left or planted it there on purpose. A message possibly, not understandable to others, but understandable to himself.'

'You're correct. A message not yet understandable to others, but it will be. It's a breakthrough. No question about it.' Chen went on after a short pause, 'Now I have studied the pictures. The mask . . . hold on, something else really strange about the mask, Yu.'

'What about it, Chief?'

'It is reminding me of a scene – something I saw just this morning – I was out for some street food . . .'

Yu knew better than to push, waiting patiently for Chen to go on.

So it was Chen's turn to give a detailed description about the street scene that morning, particularly of the sesame-strewn earthen oven cake for the young girl with her mask off. He had paid extra attention to the scene without knowing why. It was because of something in the information concerning the crime scene of Xiang's death, something raising a question in his subconscious mind, Chen now realized.

'It's also about the point you have raised regarding the mask. What was Xiang having for breakfast that morning? The earthen oven cake with the fried dough stick. For such a breakfast, people have to have it fresh and hot. Once cold, the taste would be mostly gone. Most people would start eating on the street. But how could someone have done so without taking off the mask?

'And the scene of the cake-eating girl, in retrospect, really illustrates the point. She had a mask on while waiting in front of me in the line, but once she started eating, she took the mask off. Even so, it could be a bit messy to have the sesame-strewn cake on the street, with the sesame stuck to her lips and cheeks; she had to wipe her face with a pink paper napkin.'

Chen seemed to be talking in a rather jumpy way, but Yu got his point.

With the phone still in his hand, Inspector Chen moved into the Shanghai Writers' Association, but he learned nothing new about Qiang there.

He remained in mysterious disappearance.

People were worried, but they were unable to do anything other than report it to the police bureau. And according to regulations, it was too early for the bureau to step in for an investigation. They had to wait at least another day.

So Chen had to make phone calls to someone surnamed Liao in the bureau, making sure that Qiang's name was immediately put on the missing persons' list.

'He could be drinking a cup of tea somewhere, you know,' Liao said darkly, 'for a man with sensitive information in his position.'

That was exactly what worried Chen, but he said nothing about it to Liao, nor to the people in the association.

Ouyang was out for a meeting. Chen asked some questions of Meiling instead, who seemed to be evasive, hemming and hawing, unwilling to look him in the eye.

He checked his watch. Already near twelve. It was not a day for him to spend hours on questions that seemed to be leading nowhere.

So he was ready to leave the association for the preview in the New World.

After lunch, after selecting the pictures, after sending a text message to Peiqin, Detective Yu asked Detective Qin over to his office.

With Qin focusing on the number four victim Xiang, Yu began by raising the point about her mask and cake that morning, ready to bring up Inspector Chen's analysis for support. He had hardly got into any details, however, when Qin brushed it aside, waving his second finger.

'We have noted that, Inspector Yu. But it was more than a block – not just several steps, as you have said – from the *Wenhui* building to that snack stall. So it made sense for her to pull on a mask to go there. As for the incompatibility of eating the cake and wearing the mask at the same time, Xiang could have worn the mask with just one of its straps on while biting at the cake in her hand. You may have seen young people doing that on the street. Sort of rakish among them. Nothing to wonder about.'

'Yes, it could have been like that,' Yu said, admitting to himself that he should have thought of the possibility. As a result, he found himself at a temporary loss as to how to go on discussing the other issues of the mask.

And Qin was already standing up. 'I'm going to a meeting with Internal Security again. I'll keep you posted. Don't worry about it, Inspector Yu.'

The moment Qin was out of the office, Yu began dismissing the scenario of her having the mask on with only one strap.

A young woman like Xiang could have done that. It sounded plausible in theory – but far-fetched. Yu started pacing about in the cubicle alone.

Some of the details of Inspector Chen's analysis came back to him. It would have been messy to eat the sesame-strewn cake from one's hand, not to mention the oily fried dough stick. If Xiang had kept the mask on with one strap, letting it dangle over her cheek, it could have been easily smeared, unwearable afterward.

His cellphone buzzed. It was a text message from Peiqin in response to his sent before the discussion with Detective Qin.

'I've just talked to Lianping again. Here's one detail from her about the mask – if that's what you're really focusing on.

'The snack stall is nearby. No need for a mask with such a short distance, at least that's Lianping's take. When Xiang walked out that morning, neither her colleagues in the building nor the doorman at the entrance remember seeing her wear a mask. Besides, Lianping has never seen anyone wearing a yellowing mask in *Wenhui*. She checked with Xiang's colleagues in the same section. The same impression.'

'It's unbelievable that Lianping would have done all that for the investigation.'

'Don't think she has done that for you, my husband. It's for Inspector Chen. By the way, any news about his trip to Wuxi?'

'No news, but one more question,' Yu typed back. 'If she had worn the mask to the food stall, what would she have done with it when she started eating?'

'She could have put the mask in her pocket or purse.'

'Was it possible to have the mask on by wearing only one strap around her ear?'

'What's the point of doing that? The mask would get smeared with the street food, or it could be blown away by the wind.'

'Exactly, Peiqin,' Yu typed back. 'You are really the better half of a cop.'

'Like in a favorite proverb of Old Hunter's: "When she marries a cock, go along with the cock, and when a dog, with the dog." Alas, I married a cop.'

There was no possibility of pulling pig-headed Detective Qin around, Detective Yu realized, even if he tried to talk to him again with the combined arguments of Peiqin and Inspector Chen. So Yu decided to move further along that direction by himself.

The first step was for him to find more information about the yellowish mask.

To his dismay, however, the Internet research failed to show any picture of a yellowish mask.

For his subsequent telephone inquiries, none of the pharmacy stores responded in a positive way either. Basically, they had never carried a yellowish mask. According to the salespersons, some young girls might have tried to make their masks prettier by adding flower or bird sticks, but a yellowish mask was not preferable by any standard.

Not willing to give up so easily, Yu went out to several pharmacies in person, carrying the pictures of the mask in question.

As anticipated, his police badge enabled him to get some more detailed information from the people working there, though far from close to anything like a breakthrough. 'We have carried quite a variety of masks, Officer Yu. For instance, a pinkish one with embroidered patterns was quite a hit among young girls several months ago. People could not help taking another look at them. And the "another look" effect is what they really want. But for a yellowish mask, no, I don't think so.'

'Masks are the hottest commodity on the market of late, produced by quite a number of companies, and the most popular made by 3M. The American brand, you know. Some young people even wear them as a sort of personal or political expression, depending on the occasion. But we do not carry anything yellowish. No customer would care for such a color.'

It was not until the fourth store Yu visited that a medical supply clerk studied the pictures of the masks and shook his head dubiously.

'I'm the buyer for the store, but I've never seen such a mask – except in a sci-fi movie, the name of which I forget. Some hospital may have specially ordered that, though. It looks like it's pre-treated, immersed in anti-bacterial solution.'

It flashed across Yu's mind that Peng, the first victim, had been attacked on her way from a hospital. She could have got that yellowish mask from there.

Standing outside the store, Detective Yu immediately started making inquiries with a list of hospital phone numbers *Baidued* on his cellphone.

Not exactly to his surprise, Shanghai Number One People's Hospital, the first one he contacted, confirmed that the yellowish masks had been ordered and supplied for free to staff members and in-house patients, and to the family members accompanying the patients there too. With the smoggy air, even healthy people were prone to flus, and the hospitals were particularly concerned with cross infection for the patients with low immune systems under chemotherapy.

So it was not too surprising for Peng to have a yellowish mask for herself, even though she was not really a hospital staff member.

But if that were the case, what about the third victim, and possibly the fourth? They too had the yellowish masks – possibly planted beside them.

Inspector Chen arrived at the south entrance of the New World.

He checked his watch. Still about twenty minutes before the meeting at the Oriental Club. He took a walk around the area first, pulling his gray felt beret lower, and adjusting a pair of amber-colored glasses along his nose ridge.

The Oriental was a club for the successful elite in the high-end area of the city. Chen happened to know about the place through Mr Gu, the developer, who had pushed into the inspector's hand a club membership card for free – 'in recognition of your excellent translation of the business plan, which succeeded in securing the first international loan for the New World'.

He did not see anything unusual after circling the club a couple of times.

At the club entrance stood an elderly doorman in a red uniform, smiling, bowing, who stopped Chen with his white-gloved hand raised.

'Mr Bian of the Air Product Group is sending me here as his representative,' Chen said, producing his membership card as well for something like double insurance, 'for the meeting at twelve thirty.'

'Another representative,' the doorman mumbled, casting a curious look at Chen's amber-colored glasses and waving him in without further ado.

On the first floor of the club Chen found a spacious meeting room arranged like a lecture room with a lectern and screen at the front, and rows of leather-cushioned chairs for the audience.

The room was already in semi-darkness, with the windows closed and the curtains drawn, and quite a number of people sitting in there. Chen moved to seat himself at a corner in the back, surprised at the large turnout. Thirty-five or so, possibly more by the time the meeting began. Luckily, they seemed not to be interested in making small talk with each other. Rather, they appeared to be quite cautious, saying little to each other, and none to an unfamiliar face like Chen. They knew they were going to watch a movie soon.

Less than five minutes later, a young woman came quietly in through a side door, walking straight to the lectern with a laptop satchel slung over her shoulder.

From his seat in the back he could make out only a vague profile of her in the faint light. She was wearing a trench coat over white blouse pants.

'Today's agenda is simple,' she started, speaking in a crisp voice, and taking a laptop out to the lectern. 'Preview. But mind you, it's not the final version of the documentary. There is still room for change.'

Shanshan's voice, which he immediately recognized, though it was slightly different at this moment. A note of mature confidence, he contemplated, speaking as a well-known environmental activist with millions of followers online.

She did not look in his direction, for she was leaning down to a technician beside her, who appeared busy setting up a cable connection at the lectern.

Chen was able to take a better look at her the moment the technician turned on the overhead light, which fell streaming over her face with a soft, intense transparency. She was as strikingly attractive as he remembered, her oval face framed by long black hair, vivacious with a radiance pouring out from within, a serene look in her clear, large eyes.

She said some words in an abated voice to the technician while still smiling with her mouth subtly curved, explaining some computer issues to him.

Then she turned to slip off the maroon trench coat, her long hair waving in a graceful move, which galvanized him with a sense of déjà vu.

Was it the trench coat she had worn, coming to him in the small sampan by Tai Lake that morning?

That so-long-ago morning, while waiting at the lakeside, he saw her moving through a gourd-shaped stone gate at a distance, tripping light-footed across the verdant meadow dappled in the shadow of a boxwood tree. She was dressed for the occasion, wearing a maroon trench coat of light material over a white strapless dress, and high heels. He was overjoyed with the idea that she was dressed for his company, like in a Confucian saying: 'A woman makes herself beautiful for the man who appreciates her.'

He registered the details vividly at the time. Later on, he realized it was like the scene he put – slightly modified – at the beginning of that long poem.

> *She walks in a red trench coat*
> *like a bright sail cutting*
> *through the poisonous smog*
> *enveloping the lake and its shore.*
> *Amid chemical drops from a network*
> *of corroded pipes overhead, long*
> *in disrepair, a mud-covered toad*
> *jumps upon the pollution report*
> *in her hand, opening its sleepy eyes,*
> *seeing all around still murky,*
> *slumping back to sleep . . .*

'During our previous meetings,' she resumed speaking at the lectern with the light getting dim again, 'we discussed a number of issues. We have since incorporated your suggestions into the documentary. After the preview today, we are going to have another short discussion.'

With the room falling back into darkness, the documentary began with an image of her standing in front of a larger screen, making a PowerPoint presentation. Dressed casually in jeans and a white shirt, she paced back and forth on the screen, talking, holding a pointer in her hand, combining personal narrative, investigative reporting and explanatory observations to explore the causes of the dire air pollution that was plaguing Chinese cities.

The documentary consisted of interviews, charts and scenes from different perspectives, with poor people suffering in a 'lung cancer village', environmental scientists complaining about the difficulty of enforcing regulations, the local officials mouthing about the importance of keeping up production in spite of the PM 2.5 level over ten times higher than the international standards . . .

Chen pressed the button of a mini recorder hidden in his trouser pocket. A lot of research had been done for the documentary and it was out of the question for him to remember the specific details, let alone to digest them. He knew he had to review some of them later.

In the shifting scenes of the movie, Shanshan was seen consulting scientists for explanations about why tiny particles in the ever-worsening air could prove to be particularly lethal; comforting a little Shanxi girl who said while sobbing that she had not seen a real star, nor white clouds, nor blue sky for more than half a year; conducting the research with equipment that effectively filtered out the air particles of a small room into a large bowl of pitch black water.

The movie eloquently demonstrated how China had been losing its 'battle against air pollution', though not jumping to any political conclusion. The targets of its criticism included the GDP-oriented economical practices, making examples of such state-owned mega companies as Zhonghua Petroleum Company, Petro Shengzhou, and National Petroleum & Chemical Corporation, all of them shown ruthlessly tramping the environmental regulations in their devil-may-care production. In the background, some government officials were shown collaborating with the companies, making adamant refusals to shut down those factories or productions, unable or unwilling to act in any responsible way.

Shanshan spoke in the scenes in a gentle manner, once or twice smoothing her hair with her slender hand, her silhouette seemingly too slim against those heavy contents, yet standing there full of strength, a radiance shining from her visionary passion.

The lights returned to the meeting room. She moved back to the lectern, arranging a folder as the film ended.

A short silence ensued. It was an extraordinarily eloquent, enlightening, educational and convincing documentary from its multi-perspectives and vivid details. She stood waiting for comments from the audience.

It was then that Chen came to the full realization why some high-ups, including Comrade Zhao, were so concerned about the documentary. While the film refrained from pointing fingers, an implied message was perceivable: the Party government was held ultimately responsible for the environmental disaster.

'Any questions or suggestions,' she said.

'How did you manage to do the interview with Kang, the head of Zhonghua Petroleum Company?' a white-haired man questioned. 'Did he actually allow you to record it?'

'It took a long period of time making the video, as we all know. At the time of the interview, Kang simply saw what the company did as politically justifiable, and untouchable too. He accepted my interview request only to give me a lecture, which he later used for propaganda purposes in the company newsletter. But that was at the time when the governmental accusation against the conspiracy of the American Embassy was still echoing, and with few people really aware of the disastrous consequences of the smog-smothered sky. Believe it or not, some of the scenes in the film were also provided by the interviewees those days.'

The interview in question represented Kang sitting opposite Shanshan, Chen recalled, describing the air pollution as the necessary price for the unprecedented economic development, declaring arrogantly that China had to move up to the top of the world that way.

'The whole "petroleum gang" is now in big trouble, I've heard,' the white-haired commenter chipped in again. 'Allegedly the very target of the new government's anti-corruption crackdown, with their boss Yong implicated in the background.'

Chen had heard of that too. Yong, who had risen to the pinnacle of power from an entry-level cadre in the petroleum industry, was commonly regarded as the patron of the gang in question. As a member of the powerful Politburo Standing Committee, and with that in charge of Internal Security, Yong was said to be engaged in a last-ditch battle against the new general secretary of the Central Party Committee, a Red Prince from the Forbidden City.

Chen said nothing, aware of a wave of abated whispers sweeping the room. People knew how complicated things could have been at the top.

She too said nothing for a minute, still waiting, but she appeared to be casting a glance in his direction. His was a new face in the meeting room. It would be natural for people to pay attention to a stranger there, even though it might have been nothing too uncommon for a new representative of a partner company to come sit at a preview.

With his beret pulled low, he prayed no one would recognize him. Some of the Big Bucks there might also have met him before.

People started talking about the documentary, and about things related to it. But more than anything else, about how much could prove to be too much. It made sense for them to carefully weigh the consequences. For those well-established businessmen, their businesses still had to go on as before – in the last analysis – under the leadership of the 'great, glorious and correct Chinese Communist Party'.

Judging from their discussion, Chen understood that the project was pretty much done. He was in no position to comment like some others who had been involved from the beginning. So he kept making notes, his head hung low, like a dutiful representative.

Shanshan resumed, taking a small sip from a water bottle on the lectern.

'There're a lot of factors contributing to the oppressive smog hanging over all our heads, a long list of them indeed, but only some of them are covered in the documentary.

'But I also want to ask a specific question here. Why are all of these factors coming up together in today's China? Again, a list of answers could be long – very long indeed. But one in particular, as a friend once discussed with me by Tai Lake, is the ideological crisis for the Chinese society. After the ending of the Cultural Revolution, after the exposing of numerous corruption scandals in the Party system, there seems to be nothing left for people to believe in – except what they believe they could grasp in their own hands, for which they will do anything at whatever expense, including the environmental expense.

'So it is not just about the contamination of the water, air, food, but also about the contamination of the mind.

'But that friend of mine also mentioned to me about his adherence to a Confucian principle: "There are things a man can do, and things a man cannot do." So he has no choice but to do things at risks to himself. His talk has been so inspiring to me during the making of the documentary. If each of us tries to do something we believe we can and should do . . .'

He could not help looking up. She was talking about him, who had once cited that Confucian maxim to her by the lake, though perhaps more in a reference to his cop job. She still remembered . . .

Had she recognized him?

She was looking at another audience member who was raising his hand and responding in excitement, 'Yes, after watching the documentary, people may no longer remain silent, and they will try to do something about the air pollution in whatever way they can.'

'Then, hopefully, a difference can be made.'

Several men in the audience started applauding.

'One more thing,' Shanshan was concluding. 'My husband's computer has recently been hacked. Some of his business plans mysteriously came out in a web forum. Luckily, no serious damage.'

'Why the revelation of his business plans?' A middle-aged man in a black wool suit raised the question, still clapping his hands. 'Is that web forum run by someone in competition with his business?'

'That I don't know.'

'So it could have come as a warning?'

'I don't know that either. But we all have to be careful.'

'Yes, we cannot be too careful. You're right about it,' the man in the black wool suit said, nodding, rising with several others, ready to leave.

It was almost three in the afternoon when Chen walked out of the club.

Once outside, he started looking around. He hastened over to the vine-draped veranda of a Greek restaurant, where he placed himself behind an imitation marble column, though still in view of the club entrance.

There was a new black Mercedes waiting on the club driveway, and shortly afterward, Shanshan was seen emerging with the maroon trench coat draped on her arm heading toward the car.

In the value system of today's China, he was supposed to feel happy for her – her success and wealth. The luxurious car waiting for her appeared to make a perfect match with her elevated status.

Whether it was something she really wanted, however, he could not tell.

It was ironic that he had seen her the last time in Wuxi, in a similar way, with her moving toward a car, and with him standing hidden behind a tree, unseen.

It appeared as if the current scene was conjuring up just another apparition of déjà vu all over again.

Still, there's no stepping twice into the same river, not for her, not for him.

There she was, with her chauffeur hurrying to hold the door for her, looking like a grin shining in the afternoon light.

Only she was no longer the Shanshan he had known in Wuxi, but Yuan Jing in Shanghai, an acclaimed environmental activist and an influential Internet celebrity, determined to make a difference in today's China.

As for him, he was still not able to come out into the open, to say hi to her, not even with any knowledge that he would be able to do anything for her, or for himself, an inspector being investigated by others in secret.

> *The present, when you are thinking*
> *of it, is already slipping*
> *into the past . . .*

But it was not a moment for him to let the present slip away into the past again, and he hastened to pull himself together.

The Mercedes was rolling down the driveway, with her reaching a hand out of the car window, waving to others, but not to him, who was nowhere to be seen near the club entrance.

Soon, the spring is departing again.
How much more of the wind and rain
can it endure? The cobweb alone
seems to care, trying to catch
a wisp of fading memories.
Why is the door always shut,
covered in the dust of doubts?
A dog is barking in the cell
in the distance.
Who is the one walking beside you?

Inspector Chen finally came out from behind the column, walking around like a tourist who was enjoying himself in the brave New World, instead of leaving for home.

What he had just learned in the club meeting he had to digest in concentration.

One or two minutes later, however, he came to an abrupt stop at the sight of La Maison, a French restaurant located north of the club, with the club entrance still in view.

Outside the restaurant a colorful poster showed a splendidly lit stage with a bevy of half-clad French girls dancing in the evening. For the moment, it appeared to be a fairly quiet place, with none of the tables occupied outside. Glancing in through the half-open door, Chen saw hardly any customers inside, either.

He took a table outside, sitting under the poster, like a tourist with nothing better to do than to wait for the performance at night.

A young French waitress moved toward him with a large menu. He ordered just a cup of coffee.

After placing the coffee on the table and giving him the Wi-Fi password on a slip of paper, she withdrew. He typed in the password for his phone. It was a perhaps common scene in the age of *Weibo* and *Weixin*.

He decided to do some research and to sort out the latest information. In the meantime, sitting there in front of La Maison, he would be able to keep the club entrance in sight, though he wondered whether there would be anything happening there now the meeting was over.

In spite of his determined attempt at research, his thoughts kept wandering away.

Shanshan had done a thorough job with the documentary. But for his job and reporting about it to Zhao, he did not even know how to start yet. Nor did he have the slightest mood for it at this moment. More research was needed; he once again tried to rationalize his procrastination.

He started by double-checking some of the data covered in the movie, all of which proved to be quite accurate. In addition, he ferreted out relevant articles and posts about the cancer village in question, about the increasing PM 2.5 rate in a year-by-year study, as well as other related topics, none of which showed any inaccuracy in Shanshan's presentation. It did not take long for him to be convinced that the documentary was a truly well-researched one, of which he should be able to tell Zhao.

After finishing the cup of coffee, he shifted his focus to some of the topics covered in the discussion after the preview. It was then that the 'extraordinary interview' with Kang jumped to his attention. Chen took out the mini recorder and pressed the play button.

The documentary contained only part of the interview, so its full version could be much longer. Digging into the web archive of Zhonghua Petroleum Company, Chen tried to locate that particular interview but to no avail.

It was possible that the company did not keep the newsletter it appeared in for such a long time. But after typing a combination of key search words, he succeeded in unearthing the full interview in a seemingly unrelated website.

He read the statement by Kang closely, which proved to be in accordance with the official propaganda at the time. Put in the context of the current air pollution, however, Kang's argument would have enraged a large number of audiences.

What's worse, with Yong's trouble within the Forbidden City, Kang was left in a very vulnerable position, and the release of the documentary could deliver a fatal blow to him and to the 'petroleum gang' too.

But how could people like Kang have known nothing about the documentary project? It was conceivable for a half-retired

Party leader like Zhao to have only vague ideas about it, but Kang should have learned much more, and earlier too, considering his close tie to the powerful Yong in charge of Internal Security.

Chen tapped his fingers on the table gloomily, when he found his thoughts shifting all of a sudden to what Shanshan had said toward the end of the meeting.

Her remark about her husband's computer having been hacked.

Her husband was just a businessman. On the contrary, she would have been a far more likely target for hacking because of her environmental activities.

Was it possible that they were hacking her as well as the people related to her?

That might have been the reason why she had brought up the subject in the club. A necessary reminder to the others involved in the project, though she had refrained from being too specific.

However, no one else there seemed to have been aware of anything unusual when it came to their computers. Perhaps they were not that closely related to her.

The inspector was still not in a position to put the pieces together in a comprehensive way, he supposed, since he was far from having collected all the background information about them.

Where else could he try to find the missing pieces?

But Inspector Chen was unable to concentrate long enough on any of the pieces, as Detective Yu called into his special phone.

'What's up, Yu?'

'Peiqin has just sent some *Zongzi* to Lianping, and she would like me to bring some to you as well. Dragon Festival is drawing nearer.'

'That's mouth-watering,' he said, thinking it's much more than mouth-watering. Peiqin had already had *Zongzi* delivered to him. The mention of Lianping's name could be a hint about something too much to talk about on the phone.

For a sensitive investigation, it would be too difficult for partners to discuss cases on the phone or through text messages.

'So where are you, Chief?'

'At a café in the New World. How about having a cup of coffee with me? It's a French café called La Maison, with a poster outside sporting French girls dancing a bong bong dance at night. You won't miss it.'

'You really have the leisure time for a cup of coffee . . .' But Yu too was quick to catch the cue. 'I'll be there in twenty minutes.'

Raising his hand, Inspector Chen signaled to the French waitress for another cup of coffee. This time she carried over a pot of black coffee and, after adding some into his cup, left the pot on the table.

Sipping, he thought that some snacks might help to calm his upset stomach after too much coffee. Turning around, he glanced toward the glass counter containing a variety of French bakery products near the door.

Following his glance, the waitress seated herself at a table outside, lit a cigarette, and blew out a smoke ring – likely in expectation of his making the new order. She could turn out to be one of the girls performing on the stage in three or four hours. Possibly the very glamorous one in the poster, in which she looked so unbelievably sexy. For the moment, however, she appeared a little sleepy, quite slipshod, barefoot in the discolored slippers, her golden hair disheveled though not without a suggestion of exotic charm.

It was just not her moment yet – perhaps just like an investigator finding himself clueless, still at quite a distance from the conclusion.

Then he saw another lone customer inside the café who was moving out to a wooden shelf close to the door, picking up a copy of a magazine and perching himself on a table beside, perhaps another customer waiting for the performance in the evening. Instead of opening the magazine, he was holding up a cellphone. But that cellphone holder was not talking or typing, not even reading or surfing, with his glance over the phone stealthily following the French waitress, who remained sitting there, humming to herself, her shoulder-length hair lighting up the somber wall behind, her bare toes tapping on the gray concrete ground.

It dawned on Chen. The only other customer in La Maison was taking pictures or shooting a video of the French girl in secret. Possibly a hapless lover, but more likely a third-or-fourth class paparazzi planning to sell the video of a French dancer offstage – juxtaposed with those images of her onstage – for some small amount of money.

Or perhaps not a small sum. Just about a month earlier, he had read about the scandal of a Sichuan city mayor falling out of office because of his intimate pictures with a naked girl posted online – the pictures for which his political rival paid quite a sum to a private investigator.

Was the French waitress aware of it?

Chen was not sure. For those pictures, she might not have to worry about a political scandal. On the contrary, she could be enjoying the moment of being filmed by someone's camera – not merely enamored with her glamorous role in the lime-light, but with her less glamorous moment as a tired waitress in the café.

It was none of his business, though. Chen found himself almost being the one too many there, but there seemed to be something vaguely fascinating yet at the same time disturbing about the scene, bugging illusively at the back of his mind.

Stirring the black coffee with a silver spoon, he had another thought rippling far away in his mind. Those pictures of Shanshan that Detective Huang had shown him in the Wuxi hotel.

And it was another previously missing piece that threw him into panic. All of a sudden, he began sweating profusely. It was not that an implausible scenario, which made sense in the context of other pieces.

He forgot about his stomach upset and took another large gulp from the mug.

Detective Yu was not exactly surprised at the sight of Inspector Chen enjoying a cup of coffee in the New World. Nothing could be too surprising when it came to the inspector.

'Anything new?' Chen said as soon as Yu took a seat opposite him at the outside table.

Yu went into a fairly detailed account of what he had thought and done about the mask, took a sip at the bitter coffee, before he went on with a question.

'What's the point of planting the masks at the scene? However reckless or desperate, the criminal knew it would be easier for others to trace a mask in that particular color.'

'There must have been an irresistible urge for him to leave that signature at the crime scene, an urge to make a statement, which is of supreme importance, at least to himself, and that overwhelms the safety consideration.'

'But even with such a mask as a potential clue, we still haven't got the faintest idea pointing at the possible identity of the murderer. In Lianping's latest text to Peiqin, Zhou's already been announced as a suspect inside the newspaper.'

'Peiqin and Lianping have really been texting each other a lot.'

'Since their meeting in the Longhua Temple service, Peiqin has been talking about her from time to time, saying that she owes Lianping a big one for her presence at the temple. And the two like each other. Lianping truly goes out of her way to help when Peiqin asks her for it.'

There was no immediate response from the chief inspector, and Yu changed the topic.

'But back to the case, we don't have much time left for us. The murderer will strike out again before the week is over.'

'That's true. This Friday. One victim a week. With Internal Security and Qin focusing on Zhou, we may not have the recourse to forestall such a move, even with the mask as a clue.'

'What's wrong, Chief? You are looking so pale.'

'Too much coffee, I think. Coffee sickness. Yes. You've just mentioned the Buddhist service at the temple, where Lianping and Peiqin met for the first time. You wondered at the time, I still remember, what's the point having the service, and now what's the point planting the mask at the crime scene. For some, the point is surely there, though not visible or understandable to others. Peiqin went to the temple service because of the expectations from her relatives; I went there, to be honest, in return for her help over all these years; and Lianping went there because of the article she had to write about me – perhaps a little more than that, for all I could tell. In short, people all have a reason or point for what they believe they have to do. An absolute logic for it whether conscious or subconscious. Like the beginning of *The Unbearable Lightness of Being*.'

Chen now looked ghastly pale, quite possibly more 'coffee sick' than he realized, but it was also possible he was carried away for some reason beyond Yu. When Chen went on in such a rambling, almost incomprehensible way, Yu knew from experience that ideas might have been jostling and juggling in the head of the enigmatic inspector. A monologue like that could have masked his desperate attempt to sort something out. Yu thought better of interrupting the train of his partner's thought, but he could not help stopping Chen's hand reaching out to add more coffee to his mug.

'I'm fine, Yu. Don't worry about the digression. It's just the name of a French novel I've read. It talks about people behaving in certain ways in spite of themselves, giving in to a compulsive ritual. Back to the Buddhist service at the temple. These ritualistic services are really growing in today's China. Like the banquet dedicated to the Money God, which I saw for the first time at a friend's home last month. It's in fashion for the increasingly materialistic society. For a lot of people, it's simply a must. Take my mother, for instance. It's her going vegetarian once every half a month, the fifteenth in the lunar calendar. Or once a week . . .'

Instead of rambling on, however, Chen lapsed into silence all of a sudden.

'In your notes on another serial murder case,' Yu said, after having waited for a minute for Chen to go on, 'you also talked about something like a ritual with its inner logic comprehensible only to the murderer, even though the choice of victims seemed to be so uncalled for and unrelated. But ritual or not ritual, it will be too much of a blow to the bureau when another victim falls this week. For a cycle of seven days, we have only two days left.'

'Yes, for a cycle of seven days,' Chen said, echoing, 'and he'll act before the week is over. Exactly seven days. There's a sort of ritualistic offering that Chinese families – most Chinese families – have to make after the death of a family member.'

'Seven-seven!'

'Exactly! According to the folk belief, the soul of the deceased is unwilling to leave the human world, so it lingers here, as if still functioning – at least partially functioning – like in life. Seven days after one's passing away, his or her family members will gather together for a special meal dedicated to the dead, along with the burning of candles and incense, and sometimes of the nether world money too, and then the meal will be enjoyed by the living family members, like in a family reunion with the deceased. The ritual will be repeated on the next seventh day, until the end of the seventh week. By that time, the soul of the deceased is said to be able to leave in contentment. With the deceased so far away from home at the end of the seven weeks, the family does not have to provide the ritual service any more, though some still do so, like at a hundred-day anniversary, or ten-year anniversary, or some other variation.'

'Yes, Peiqin has told me about it. The service at Longhua Temple was the twenty-year ritual for Peiqin's parents having left the world, more or less the same logic as with the seven-seven.'

'So the murderer strikes out at a seven-day interval.'

'That's true, but not exactly at a seven-day interval. Let me double check,' Yu said in a hurry, taking out his phone to pull out a chart. 'Eight days between the first and second, six days between the second and the third, and then seven days.'

'That's more than understandable, I think, if we take into consideration the difficulty of his killing exactly on the seventh day at those central locations. After all, to commit the crime may not be as easy as to prepare a meal at home. The killing of the second victim might not have been performed on the seventh day for some unforeseeable reason, given the circumstances. So he had to act on the following day. Then for the third victim, it was after six days – to average it to seven days.'

'That's right. So you're really talking about the scenario of a sociopath killing for the ritual of seven-seven this coming Friday?'

'Unless with some unpredictable factors, one day more or less, for the cycle of seven.'

'Friday or Saturday, there's not much time left for us,' Yu repeated himself, wringing his hands.

'Now the rationale of the seven-seven is about some special offering to the deceased. My mother used to go to the food market so early in the morning, I remember, for a special meal – at least with fish and meat, and father's favorite Yunnan ham too – on the seventh day for seven weeks. And that along with the nether world money, the incense, the candles and what not. In short, some really special offering for the deceased.'

'In other words, the murderer simply takes other lives as special ritualistic offerings to the deceased. Certainly way more special than an exceptional meal. So he will at least take three more lives – to the end of the seven-seven – before coming to a stop. What can we do?'

'That being the case,' Chen said, refilling his mug, 'we may start checking for somebody who died – quite possibly unfair, as seen in the murderer's mind – seven days before the appearance of Peng's body near the Bund. That may be a long shot, but worth trying.'

'But it's not an easy job for such a large city. More than hundreds of people die on a single day.'

'We can try to narrow it down,' Chen said, with a sudden edge in his voice. 'Let's start with hospitals.'

'There're a number of hospitals, too.'

'It's possible to narrow it down further. For the present case, as we have discussed, we have reasons to assume the murderer is a young or middle-aged man, capable of killing with speed and force, knowledgeable about how to stay out of the way of the patrolling cops and the surveillance cameras; and the dead, a woman closely related to him, about the same age. That's what pushed him over the edge.'

'Anything else for the profile?'

'In his mind, the tragedy should not have happened. Medical

malpractice, for instance. Considering the first victim was from a hospital too, we may look into that very hospital.'

'It's so logical, Chief. Medical disputes make so many headlines online and off in today's society. In the light of it, the first victim being one from the hospital also makes sense. It's brilliant, that deduction of yours, Inspector Chen.'

'No, it's you that have drawn my attention to it. The yellowish mask from the hospital, though it may be something different from a medical dispute.'

'I'll be damned, Chief. I have to go to the hospital right now.'

'Yes, I have to leave too,' Chen said. 'For a good meal with an old friend.'

Staring at his boss, Yu said instead, 'Come on, Chief Inspector Chen. You are sounding more and more like an impossible gourmet.'

As Detective Yu was leaving the café, Inspector Chen glanced at his watch. Quite a while had elapsed since the ending of the preview. With nothing suspicious detected at the club entrance, he saw no point staying any longer at the café.

There was something more urgent for him to do.

He started moving toward the southern exit of the New World, where he noted a number of new restaurants, one of which showed a large 'organic' sign in the front with a smaller line underneath saying 'private room for two'. He took a picture of the sign, like a card-carrying gourmet.

Once out of the New World, Chen started looking for a public phone booth, but the area was too new, too luxurious for the existence of an outdated phone booth. It was not until after making a couple of turns that he spotted one in a small street. Glancing over his shoulder, he stepped in, closed the door and dialed the number of Melong, a 'retired' hacker.

'Hi Melong, it's me, another unfilial son under the sun.'

'Oh, another unfilial son . . .' Melong sounded instantly alert, recognizing Chen's voice in the context known to them alone. 'But I'm the truly unfilial son, not you. Anyway, what's up?'

'I've just walked past an organic restaurant in the New World, and I'm thinking of you as a pro on organic food. How about we have a delicious but healthy meal today? The restaurant is near the southern entrance of the New World. I can send you a picture of it with the address. It's long time no see for the two of us.'

'Long time no see indeed. But don't be sucked in by those expensive restaurants in the New World. They simply rip off in the name of organic. I happen to know a restaurant that is definitely organic. Let's go there. It's on Tongchuan Road. Called Small River. You won't miss it. My treat. Six thirty.'

'Tongchuan Road?'

Chen had been to one of the restaurants there, which were known because of a live fish market on the same street, with stalls aligned in front of the restaurants. Customers could choose their favorite sea or river food in the market, which the chef would then have prepared and cooked in whatever way they liked. Fresher, cheaper, and also tastier.

But organic? Chen had never heard anything about it in connection to those restaurants.

'Yes, it will be a yummy surprise for you. That much I can guarantee you, but I'll say no more for now.'

'See you then, Melong.'

The subway train to Tongchuan Road was so crowded, Chen had a hard time standing still, holding on to the railing overhead. More than half of the passengers there were young, wearing large masks which made their breathing even harder in the cramped space. Still, they were busy talking or typing or reading on their cellphones, as if unperturbed.

People, like some passengers in the train, were simply getting used to the 'new norm', as it was called in the media. Officially, however, it was in reference to the beginning of the slowed-down economy.

He took out his phone, seeing on the screen a chart indicating the air pollution level for the day as dangerously high – with the AQI index even worse than when one stands right behind a diesel engine exhaust.

Thinking of what he had to discuss with Melong, he bookmarked the chart.

And he could not help thinking about what he had just discussed with Detective Yu.

Was it possible that the yellowish mask from the hospital had been planted as a protest against the air pollution? If so, what was the connection to the scenario he had developed out of the seven-seven ritual?

There were still a lot of questions unanswered, but he had a hunch that it was connected to the environmental crisis in a way not known to him yet.

All the more urgent for a documentary like Shanshan's to be released for millions and millions of people to see.

With his back pressed against a pole in the packed train, he typed out a short message to Zhao.

'Have talked to a number of people about the air pollution, and heard several satirical jokes. One reads like this: *A CCTV journalist tried to interview people on the street about the pollution problem, "What kind of effect do you think the smog has on your life, Auntie?" The interviewee snapped back, "Too disastrous an effect, you cannot even see through the smog, I'm your Uncle!"*'

It's a joke he had heard among the audience in the Oriental Club.

On second thought, he composed another text message, shorter, with just one sentence, but much more serious: 'While doing the investigation under your guidance, I think I've been followed.'

In *The Thirty-Six Stratagems*, number thirteen is called 'to beat the bushes to startle out the snake'. He had no idea as to where the snake might be hiding, but Zhao might have, so he would start beating for the inspector.

Small River turned out to be a two-story restaurant with several large red lanterns dangling over its door, decorating the façade in a rather vulgar way. Apparently not a fancy restaurant like those in the New World. With several of the stalls in front sporting fish still gasping and shrimp still jumping in wooden or plastic pails and basins, the restaurant presented a shabby, slippery, sordid entrance.

Chen stepped in cautiously, looking around for Melong in the dining hall on the first floor, where a middle-aged man rose from behind the front desk and approached him.

'So you're Melong's friend? Follow me. The private room upstairs. The best one in our restaurant. By the way, my name is Chang.'

'A private room?' Melong must have made the reservation, Chen realized. The place appeared so packed and plain, the wooden floor squeaky and sticky with the drippings from the plastic bags customers carried in, and with a not-too-pleasant tang continuously wafting in from the fish market.

'Yes, follow me.'

But the private room turned out to be quite a dainty one, with a silk scroll of traditional Chinese landscape on the wall, and a bouquet of chrysanthemums in a shapely vase on the windowsill.

Chen had hardly seated himself when Melong burst into the room, carrying an extra-large black plastic bag in his hand, striding straight over to him.

'Finally you're here, Melong. We are expecting you like the most welcome rain after a prolonged summer drought,' Chang said in excitement, pouring out the tea for the two of them.

'Today is all for my distinguished friend, Mr Chen. Tell you what, his presence is an unbelievable honor to your place. Do your absolute best tonight, Manager Chang.'

'Don't worry about it. Nothing but your favorites. Wild turtle steamed with Jinhua ham and rock sugar, Asian carp fried with green onion, the seasonal vegetable in the free-range chicken broth, and we have the Japanese rice, superior quality, that's usually reserved for my own family only.' Chang added, scratching his head with a suggestion of embarrassment, 'What have you brought us today, Melong?'

'Everything you can dream of. Live wild turtles, needless to say, live fish and fresh vegetables too,' Melong said, casting a glance at the plastic bag at his foot. As if on some mysterious cue, something seemed to start twitching in the bag. 'Far more than usual today.'

'How can I ever thank you enough, my savior?' Chang scooped up the bag in his hand. 'Indeed you have saved my neck again. A super Big Buck has just called in, insisting on the Small River special – the real wild turtle.'

'What's all this about?' Chen said, baffled with the dialogue between Melong and Chang as the latter moved out of the room carrying the plastic bag.

'About the turtles in the bag. The real turtle, not farm-fed with drugs and what not. So there's a whole world of difference in the taste. And in the yin/yang boost to your body system, too. Do you think I'm here for the stuff from the smelling fish market outside? No, no way. You know I know better. For all the stories about the organic food, people immerse shrimp in formalin for better color, feed rice paddy eels with antibiotics, and so on and so forth. All things are imaginable in China. Not to mention all the chemical waste in the rivers and lakes. It's suicidal to eat such toxic food.'

'But what's the big deal between the restaurant and your black plastic bag?'

'It's a long story. Because of my mother's lung operation, and thanks to your help, the good doctor in the East China Hospital successfully operated on her in time.'

'Don't mention that again, Melong. I just gave him a phone call.'

'A phone call from the legendary chief inspector made all the difference in the world. Anyway, after the operation, she's still frail and vulnerable, liable to infection because of her low immune system. With so many healthy people having respiratory problems because of the horrible air, I was worried about her. Thanks to the sum the government paid for the unannounced control of my web forum, I was able to buy the villa in the suburbs for her recovery. And I was lucky enough to have a large backyard attached to the property – between you and me – in return for a special favor I had done for the developer.'

'For a special favor of a hacking job?'

'No worry about the devilish details, my Chief Inspector Chen. Suffice it to say that all the cogwheels for today's society are oiled with the exchange of favors. Back to the backyard. There are so many articles online about the importance of organic food, I planted some of her favorite vegetables there. No chemical fertilizer or weed killer.'

'What a filial son!'

'I also learned there's something else especially beneficial to a patient in recovery like my mother. The wild turtle. It's all yin, natural yin in the light of the traditional Chinese yin/yang medical theory. And she happens to like the turtle soup. So I dug out a small pond in the backyard and started to raise the wild turtle and fish in it.'

'Wild turtles can be quite expensive in the market, I know, but I don't think you have to worry about money.'

'Well, the turtles in the market are claimed to be wild, but it's an open secret that they are fed with antibiotics and hormones. In contrast, I stock the pond with nothing but the good and natural feed. I cannot vouch for their "miraculous effect" like in some articles, but my mother has been doing fine for a woman of her age, especially after a large operation. It is not necessarily just because of the organic turtle or vegetables, but they may have helped a little.'

'You're talking like a Suzhou opera singer today, Melong, full of suspenseful turns and digressions. But what led you to this restaurant here?'

'I'm coming to it, Chief Inspector Chen. You know I'm no chef. No way for me to prepare a live turtle that bites like crazy. So Chang, the owner of this restaurant, offered to prepare them along with other dishes for me. In return, he gets from me the "authentic" wild turtle. They became a well-known special for the restaurant.'

'And also quite a profitable sideline for you, Melong.'

'After selling the website to the Party authorities, I've washed my hands of my hacking business, as I told them – unless they want me to, you know that. I don't have to really worry about money, but making a little more now and then won't hurt. Also a good idea to let people know I'm busy with something – hacking a turtle's head.'

'You don't have to tell me a Liu Bei-like story in the *Romance of the Three Kingdoms*, about your being a meticulous, law-abiding man with no secret work going on. It's none of my business whether you're hacking a turtle's head or something else. But given your once status in the field, you may be able to find out something for me—'

Their talk was interrupted by Chang's reappearance with a silver tray holding several dishes: cold tofu mixed with wild shepherd's purse blossom, white shrimp in saltwater, fried carp head, slices of thousand-year egg in soy sauce seasoned with minced tender ginger.

'All organic,' Chang said, smiling a proud smile before withdrawing and closing the door behind him.

'What do you want me to do, Chief Inspector Chen?' Melong said, picking up a piece of the slippery ginger-covered thousand-year egg with his chopsticks.

'You must have heard of the latest, perhaps the most notorious, sex scandal video posted online, Melong.'

'You mean the video of Geng and his massage girl who later became his wife?'

'Yes, but she was murdered just a couple of days ago.'

'I've heard of something about it too in connection to the video put online.'

'It could have been hacked.'

'Its contents hacked from Geng's computer? Well, that would be something like an old lecher's collection in a Sherlock Holmes story. It's possible, but for Geng to have it taped in a massage room? I don't know. He could have easily had a girl do whatever he pleased at home instead of a massage parlor. Too much of a risk for a Party cadre like Geng. Besides, there are secret cameras installed in those clubs or massage places, as you may have heard.'

'So you mean the club videotaped the two of them without their knowledge?'

'I think I've heard stories like that. Nowadays you can never tell who's behind those clubs. Geng's powerful, but he must have his adversaries too. I'll double-check it for you if it's needed for your investigation.'

'That could be really helpful.'

'Our circle is not that large. It should not be too difficult to find out.'

'And there's another favor I have to ask of you. Sort of related. It's about a young woman named Shanshan. Some people might be trying to hack into her computer, possibly into the computers of the people close to her as well. Supposing that's the case, do you think you may be able to detect any buzz about it in your circle?'

'You mean someone is hacking her, and the people related to her too?'

'Yes, that's a possibility. Her husband's computer has recently been hacked, but hers is a far more likely target. It may just be a hunch on my part.'

'You have any specific clues?'

'No,' he said. It was out of the question for him to share the bits and pieces accumulated over the last few days.

'But for what reason are people hacking her?'

'She's an environmental activist, making a self-funded documentary about the air pollution in China. Such a documentary will not be pleasant to the government. Devious plots could have been attempted against her,' Chen said in earnest, taking out a copy of *Shanghai Literature*. 'We met in Wuxi, where I wrote the poem about the contaminated Tai Lake in her company. Now she's making a documentary here about the polluted air, and I don't want any harm to come to her.'

'You don't have to say any more,' Melong said, standing up, letting the slice of darksome egg slip splashing back into the saucer of soy sauce. 'I'll be damned.'

'What do you mean, Melong?'

'Your friend is doing the right thing, and so are you. But what about me? Catching and eating turtles like a contented fool,' Melong said bitterly. 'My mother had lung cancer, you know that. She never smoked, not once in her life. It's all because of the murderous air pollution. But for your invaluable help, she might not even have had the surgery in time.'

'You're mentioning that again, Melong, but the air pollution is a serious problem to our people.'

'Yes, the Party government has been declaring for years that the people's right to live should be far more important than the human rights as advocated in the West. But what about the rights to have the clean air, the unpolluted water, the healthy food? You must have heard stories of high-ranking Party officials having for themselves the special water and food supply that's not contaminated. And imported fresh air machines installed everywhere within the Forbidden City.'

'Not just within the Forbidden City. Wherever they go, the

fresh air machines will be installed into their hotel rooms, too. I had a talk with Comrade Party Secretary Zhao at the Hyatt Hotel just the other day. I know.'

Melong eyed him questioningly, refraining from raising a question about it.

Chen moved on with the necessary background information for Melong, who listened attentively, not interrupting him a single time.

When Chen was nearly done, Chang came in with the special dishes in addition to a bottle of Maotai brewed in the early sixties.

Melong raised the cup with an exaggerated 'Wow,' and Chen readily joined him.

Indeed it was a lavish banquet. The fish immersed in Shaoxing wine tasted tender and delicious. The monstrous turtle steamed with Jinhua ham and rock sugar in a bamboo steamer was finished in the midst of Chen's delighted exclamations. Whether it was because of the psychological effect produced by Melong's elaboration about the organic food or not, it was a palatable surprise.

'Don't worry, Chief Inspector Chen,' Melong said with a flushed face when ready to leave. 'You know you can count on me.'

In the growing dusk, Detective Yu was walking out of the hospital with heavy steps, taking a deep breath, when his cellphone started to ring. It was Peiqin.

'Anything new?'

'I've just learned something from Shanghai Number One People's Hospital where Peng, the first victim of the serial murder case, worked as a night caregiver.'

'Yes?'

'Not only was it confirmed that the yellowish mask came from the very hospital, but also that there's a patient who died there, exactly seven days prior to Peng's death.'

'Really! But what connects the two?'

'What connects the two dots, to use Inspector Chen's words,' Yu said, unwilling to withhold the credit, 'may be the very point the murderer tried to make.'

'I'm so confused. Please explain. After all, I'm a cop's wife, not a cop.'

So Yu told her briefly about the discussion he had had with Chen in the New World, and then about the subsequent visit to the hospital.

'Seven days before Peng's death, a female patient named Shen died in the hospital. Quite young. Only in her early thirties. No medical dispute whatsoever. When she was admitted into the hospital, she was diagnosed with lung cancer of the fourth stage. She and her husband Lou knew her days were numbered. Still, the two fought a hard battle to the bitter end.

'According to the doctors and nurses in the hospital, Lou has been an extraordinary husband who, in spite of his day job, came to the hospital to sit by her bed almost every night for the first month, until he himself collapsed with over-exhaustion. But even then he managed to come to the hospital every morning before going to work, and to stay by her bed at least two or three nights a week. He paid all the hospital bills on time until the last two weeks of her life. It's not easy, considering the mounting medical expense. No medical dispute whatsoever—'

'I'm still so confused, Yu.'

'Yes, there're a lot of questions unanswered. I think I'm going to Zabei Park neighborhood committee right now.'

'What for?'

'Perhaps I'll be able to answer some of your questions back home. Lou lives close to the park, and the neighborhood committee may be able to tell me a thing or two about him.'

'But it's too late. No one will be in the neighborhood office.'

'I just want to give it a try. Time really matters. You don't have to wait for me.'

Later that night, still under the influence of Maotai, Chen received another phone call from Ouyang.

Still no news about Qiang yet. People in the association were getting really worried. They'd come up with all sorts of speculations. At the insistence of Qiang's wife, they contacted the police bureau again regarding the missing persons' list, but nothing reported so far matched Qiang's appearance.

Qiang had gotten into trouble not because of anything he had done wrong, Chen contemplated. The only thing possibly suspicious at all on the part of Qiang, as far as Chen could see, was perhaps his talk with Chen at the café instead of in the office.

But their conversation could not have been recorded at the café, with so many people coming and going there and talking to each other or talking on their phones, and with Dvořák's 'New World' playing in the background. If such a talk there had raised the alarm for the people prowling in the dark, it had to be because of Chen.

So Qiang was compelled to come clean to Internal Security because of the inspector. And until Internal Security believed they had got everything out of him about the talk in the café, Qiang had to remain disappeared, drinking one cup of tea after another.

Possibly because of the inspector's connection with Shanshan as well.

Or possibly even his connection with Zhao?

Zhao was not without his adversaries at the top, Chen knew. But for such a senior Party leader in semi-retirement, it was hardly conceivable for anything to happen to him at this juncture, which could have shattered the 'political stability' advocated in the *People's Daily*.

Chen drank a large cup of instant coffee, trying to keep himself thinking clearly before composing another text message to Zhao.

'Managed to sneak into a meeting with Yuan Jing and her associates. She turned out to be someone I met in Wuxi, but long out of touch, she did not recognize me there. They were discussing what they could do for the air pollution, about the responsibility of large companies like Zhonghua Petroleum Company, and about the people who backed them. More to follow tomorrow.'

Zhao had most likely known about Shanshan's project as well as her being the heroine in his poem. So the text message would have served as proof that the inspector was throwing himself into the investigation and keeping nothing from Zhao.

As for any other details about the meeting at the club, he

did not know what to say. The promise about 'more to follow' might prove reassuring to Zhao for the moment. As for the mention of Zhonghua Petroleum Company and the people behind it, it was intended as another indirect push in 'the right direction', hopefully, as mentioned in Zhao's earlier text message.

But the inspector still had no clue regarding what he could possibly do for Qiang. He gulped at the second cup of instant coffee, hardly tasting it.

He rose to open the window. In the distant sky, the stars too seemed to be chilly, dim.

Two lines from the Qing dynasty poet Huang Zhongze came flashing back to mind, unexpectedly.

> *Alas, tonight is not last night, for all the sparkling*
> *   stars,*
> *For whom I stand out long, long against chilly dew*
> *   drops?*

He was missing Shanshan.

But he became aware of getting 'drunk' with coffee again, feeling suddenly sick in the stomach and sweating profusely. The window under the lamplight showed a pale face staring out vacantly into the night.

The memory of that far away night surged back in the dark, intensely, illuminating him in fragmented remembrances at the unlikely hour . . .

With the intensity of their passion accentuated by a touch of desperation that affected them both, they were aware there was no telling what would then happen – to her, to him, to the world. Nothing for them to grasp except the fleeting moment of being, losing, and finding themselves again in each other's arms for the present.

With her above him, she turned into a dazzling white cloud, languid rolling, soft yet solid, sweeping, almost insubstantial, clinging, pressing and shuddering when she came, then into a sudden rain, incredibly warm yet cool, splashing, her long hair cascading over his face like torrents, washing up sensations he had never known before. Then she undulated under him like the lake, ever-flowing, rising and falling in the dark, arching up, her hot wetness engulfing him, rippling, pulling him down to the depth of the night, and bearing him up to the surface again, her legs tightening around him in waves of prolonged convulsion.

Afterwards, they lay quietly in each other's arms, languorous, in correspondence with the lake water lapping against the shore, lapping in the quietness of the night.

'We're having the lake to ourselves.'

'Yes, we're the lake,' she whispered a throaty agreement before falling asleep in his arms . . .

A night bird hooted eerily, not too far away. Possibly an owl, which seemed to be quite a rarity in this increasingly mega-metropolitan city. It was supposedly unlucky at the late hour. An inexplicable sense of foreboding brought him back to the role of an inspector standing at the end of his rope, alone, in the dark.

DAY FOUR
THURSDAY

Early Thursday morning, Inspector Chen woke up suffering from a splitting headache, what with so many cups of coffee the previous night, and with the 'wild turtle' the previous day, which must have thrown the yin/yang disastrously out of balance in his body.

But it could only make the headache worse, he knew, to lie tossing and turning in bed and doing nothing.

He rose, made a pot of strong black tea, and started working on a draft of the report to Comrade Secretary Zhao.

Short, vague text messages would no longer be enough for the senior Party leader. Chen had promised 'more to follow'. There was no putting it off any more.

It would not be too difficult for him to produce an objective report about the documentary, but as for Zhao's possible reaction to it, Chen thought he could guess.

For him, what was the report trying to achieve at this stage?

However hard he might try to go through the stratagems in *The Thirty-Six Stratagems*, none seemed to be enough to win Zhao over to Shanshan's side.

In impotent frustration, he took out the magazine again, as if in an attempt to get some inspiration from those lines written by the side of Shanshan.

The broken metal-blue fingernails
of fallen leaves clutching
into the barren bank, the rotten fish
afloat on the water, shimmering
with their mercury-filled bellies,
their glassy eyes still flashing
the last horror at the apparition
of a black-bikinied witch dancing

with her raven hair streaming
on her alabaster shoulders, hopping
from the woods of the plant chimneys.
Who's the one walking beside you?

Coincidentally, it happened to be a stanza full of horror. The moment he put it down, however, another thought came across his mind.

The horror of the yellow mask serial murder case.

What could the murderer be doing at this moment?

And for that matter, what could Detective Yu be doing right now?

Last night, Yu had texted him about the discovery at the hospital, particularly concerning a patient named Shen who'd died seven days earlier than Peng, the first victim in the case, and her devastated husband Lou. These could prove to be potential leads, but no more than that at the moment.

Chen wished he had been able to give Detective Yu some more help in the investigation.

Sighing, the sickly inspector ended up swallowing a couple of pills for the worsening headache. Perhaps no help any time soon, he frowned with the knowledge.

To his dismay, the pills began to make him feel drowsy and depressed, and he dosed off in spite of himself, his head rested on the desk, beside the report with only a couple of lines written.

Shortly after five in the morning, Detective Yu found himself standing in view of Lou's apartment in Zabei District. It was not a new residential complex, built at least twenty years earlier, but nonetheless 'modern' compared to some others in the area.

The only thing for him to do there, Yu thought, was to wait on the street corner, keeping the apartment building closely in sight.

Fortunately, there was a twenty-four-hour dumpling eatery on that particular corner. So he seated himself at a table near the entrance, ordered a bowl of shrimp and pork dumplings, and started eating slowly.

Afterward, he lit a cigarette without rising from the table. At the early time, the sleepy old waiter did not mind a lone customer sitting a little longer there.

Yu saw several middle-aged women walking past the eatery in a hurry carrying bamboo baskets or plastic bags in their hand. Most likely heading to a food market nearby for the fresher food early in the morning. For the fast-changing city of Shanghai, some old conventions lingered on in spite of the considerable number of new supermarkets.

Still, nothing seemed to be happing in front of the apartment building. Yu began to smoke a second cigarette. It was almost five twenty-five. For the previous cases, all of them had happened before or around six. It would take Lou – if he was the one – at least twenty minutes to get to one of those locations to commit a horrific crime.

The old waiter came over to take away the empty bowl. It was almost five thirty.

So was Lou not the one after all? Yu crushed out the cigarette in the dented ashtray ready to leave in just another two or three minutes.

Then the door of the apartment building across the street opened and a man stepped out. After taking a quick look around, he began trotting like a morning jogger under the still gray sky.

It looked like Lou, and Yu thought he recognized him from the picture he had obtained from the neighborhood committee the night before.

Running in the smoggy morning did not seem practical to Detective Yu, but it fitted with the pattern of the murderer.

Still, it was open to question whether the jogger – if he was none other than Lou – would make it to one of those central locations before six in accordance with the established time pattern of the serial murder.

Yu rose from the table and followed him at a distance in silence. To his surprise, the jogger seemed to be already slowing down.

There was something strange about it. The man jogged for only three or four minutes. The moment he turned the street corner, he shifted pace to a leisured stroll, looking around, moving along with his hands in his trouser pocket.

He then made his way into the subway station for Line 11. No morning jogger would get on a train after running for just a few minutes.

Yu hastened his steps and got into the train after the man in question. Once in the train, he managed to take a few pictures of the man with his cellphone. Even so early in the morning, there were quite a number of passengers sitting or standing with a phone in their hand, so it was not something suspicious for Yu to do. Five minutes later, however, the man moved out in haste and changed to Line 10. Again, Yu did the same.

Shortly afterward, both of them got off at the New World station.

It was getting even weirder. The New World was a high-end shopping complex for the successful elite in the city. Yu had had coffee with Inspector Chen here the day before. It was too early, however, for shoppers and visitors.

Why should the jogger – if that was what Lou was, after all – have come all this way, taking one subway train and changing to another, to the New World? It did not make any sense. The New World was, if anything, not an area for jogging.

But the man was turning into a jogger once again, slower now, more like one walking at a relatively quick pace. He was obviously up to something, but it was already past six twenty.

For a plausible scenario, Yu thought frantically, the man was out there for reconnaissance. Today might not necessarily be the day. The murderer had to familiarize himself with the surroundings first. That was probably why he did not have to worry about the established time pattern.

And the choice of the New World, another central location of the city, made sense too. Historically, it was in one of the *shikumen* houses here that the Chinese Communist Party had held its first national conference. After the first four cases in other central locations, the New World certainly made a justifiable spot.

Jogging on, the man seemed to suddenly quicken his steps and move close to a middle-aged man in front, dangerously close, but instead of making any attempt, he turned away, and several minutes later, closed in on an elderly woman with a limp. Still, he did not try to do anything.

People were beginning to show up in the New World. The lights of the Starbucks at its north entrance turned on, almost time for the arrival of its earliest customers.

The man was turning round again and retracing his steps to the Line 10.

Yu moved behind at a cautious distance until the man disappeared into the crowd at the subway station.

At least there was no time for him to strike out that morning. Too late. It was already six twenty. A serial murderer would have closely followed the established time pattern.

There were a lot of things still beyond the detective, but he thought that the murderer would come back to the New World the next day. And most likely much earlier.

Chen was awoken by a shrill sound, like a cricket moaning in the first chilly wind of the fall. It turned out to be the ringing of that special cellphone of his.

Rubbing his eyes, he saw the light streaming in through the window. It was seven twenty-five. There appeared a weird text message on the phone screen:

'Another monstrous live turtle for two of us there. Eleven o'clock.'

The message came from Melong, who was moving quickly. And cautiously, too.

For a notorious gourmet like Chen, an invitation to a turtle meal – even if the message was intercepted – would not have sounded suspicious.

But what it really conveyed to him, the inspector knew only too well. Melong must have got something specific – too specific for him to talk about on the phone.

The sickly inspector had no choice but to go there, but he still had some time, so he tried to make another attempt at the report after taking two more pills for his badly upset stomach.

Standing in front of the crowded station, Detective Yu started typing a text message.

'A man from Lou's apartment building came out early this morning, jogging for a few minutes before taking subway trains to the New World, and jogging around there for a while before he headed back. I followed him all the time, and—'

He stopped typing. He was going to say it was the husband of the patient named Shen who'd passed away in the hospital seven days before the death of the first victim.

But things were suspicious, and Inspector Chen too must have a lot on his plate. Yu decided to do something more on his own before he would send the message to the inspector so early in the morning. Chen had looked so sick at the café, and Yu did not think it really had a lot to do with coffee.

So Detective Yu decided to go to the neighborhood committee with the pictures in his cellphone.

Around seven fifty, Detective Yu arrived at the office of Zabei Park neighborhood committee again.

It was still early, but luckily enough one retiree neighborhood activist there was capable of getting several of the committee members into the office for him. Yu was able to show the pictures he had just taken of the morning jogger to them. They immediately confirmed it was Lou.

Sitting around the long desk in the office, they were very cooperative, each of them trying to say something about what he or she knew regarding Lou. With their permission, Yu put a mini recorder on the desk so that he could listen more carefully later. If need be, he could also give a copy to Chen, though he wondered whether the inspector might have the time for it.

'The Lous have lived in our neighborhood for less than a year. Newly married, they passed around wedding candies in the building, amiable to all the neighbors there. But Lou's been a changed man since his wife got sick.'

'That's understandable for the newly married husband. Just about a month after their moving in, the wife was admitted into hospital. Heartbroken, he was heard crying like a baby at night! And he has been making an unbelievably big deal of the seven-seven ritual for her, spending money like water for the meal dedicated to her.'

'He behaves as if it's the end of the world for him. According to a neighbor in his building, he has shut himself up in the room since her death, mourning with her pictures against his bosom for hours, and hardly coming out. Not even for the work at the company. In a matter of time he'll lose his job. It cannot go on like that. Neighbors are sympathetic toward him.'

'Well, things may not have been that dramatic. According to his next-door neighbor, once or twice, he has been seen jogging early in the morning. So he's trying to recover from it.'

'But he's not his normal self. I went to his apartment to express the condolence on behalf of our neighborhood committee, but he hardly talked to me, murmuring something inexplicable with such a vacant look in his eyes.'

'A walking corpse, he's finished together with her.'

The Zabei Park neighborhood committee basically confirmed what Yu had learned about Lou in the hospital. A heartbroken man, but nothing really suspicious or strange for a husband who had just lost his beloved wife.

If anything, it backed up the part of the scenario that for such a grief-wrecked man, Lou could have been pushed over the edge.

As Inspector Chen labored up to the second floor of that red-lantern-decked Small River restaurant, Chang hurried over to him with a broad grin and pointed toward the same private room.

Melong was already waiting in there, standing up on Chen's entrance. There was no plastic bag visible on the floor, just a pot of tea with two cups beside a laptop on the table.

'Absolutely no disturbance today. I've told Chang about it. Don't worry,' Melong said, turning to lock the private room door. 'But I have to make it quick.'

'Yes?'

'Your hunch is right, Chief Inspector Chen. Someone has been hacking your friend Shanshan, and in fact, doing much more than that.'

'How did you find out?'

'The number of people doing reputable business in our line is not that large. As a rule, we do not talk much among ourselves, and it's understandable, you know, for the confidentiality of our clients. For these deals, the less said the better. If one of us asks for some specific help in the inside circle, however, one usually gets the responses needed. After all, each of us may be limited to his or her own expertise, and we have to help each other from time to time.

'Last night, I made no more than five or six phone calls before I learned something from a guy named Rong. I helped him with a project about two months ago, so he did not hesitate to tell me that he had been recently given a job – not from the government, but from someone in Zhonghua Petroleum Company, one of the largest government-run companies in the country – to make a video about your friend Shanshan. An incredibly lucrative job, for which the client offered two hundred thousand yuan, but Zhonghua Petroleum Company is so obscenely rich, no worry about the expense.'

'Wow, Zhonghua Petroleum Company. Go on.'

'It's a video about her personal life. With scenes and pictures from surveillance cameras or computers provided by the client. Rong had to hack into her computers for more, and into those of the people related to her too, as you have suspected. Some of her hacked email content may be used as part of the video – more authentic in her own words, as specially requested by the client. Rong has already edited quite a large number of the images from the surveillance cameras, but he's still working on the hacked material. It may take a couple of days before he will be able to turn in the finished product to his client.'

Melong took out of his jacket pocket a flash memory stick and inserted it into the laptop. But the moment he did this, he stood up abruptly, stealing a look at Chen before he pressed the play key, saying with a touch of unease in his voice, 'I have to make several phone calls in my business circles, sorry about that, but I'll be back in about forty-five minutes. You can lock the door. I'll knock when I come back.'

Chen had a strong foreboding about the reason why, all of a sudden, Melong had to make those business phone calls.

With the private room door locked, the video started on the laptop screen – for Inspector Chen alone.

Apparently, the video had not yet been properly edited. Its contents seemed to cover quite a long period of time, which started about five or six years ago, judging by the dates printed on some of the images in the beginning section.

It began with scenes evidently captured by a hidden camera, which represented fragmented scenes of Shanshan staying with a man in his bedroom. Some of the scenes turned out to be quite explicit. Chen took in a deep breath, watching their intimate moments, but he recognized neither the man nor the room. The date was earlier than the inspector's vacation in Wuxi.

It was hard for him to be sitting there as a detached viewer. He was confounded by the identity of the man who was holding her tight, but then he saw the light as the caption appeared underneath the scene:

'What a shameless slut who's sleeping around, even with a married criminal!'

So the man in the scene must have been Jiang, another environmental activist who had been sentenced to years, a prey to a government set-up.

What the video drove at, however, was not fair to Shanshan. At the time, she'd had no idea that Jiang had not been divorced yet. Huang, the young cop in Wuxi, had confirmed that.

In those clippings from Zhao's folder, Shanshan was generally seen by her online followers as a courageous public intellectual fighting for an idealistic cause, so the video could go a long way to destroying such an image. In China, a sensational story about the extramarital affair of a public figure, once put on the Internet, could instantly attract millions of viewers in the age of *WeChat* and *Weibo*. The viewers would be without the knowledge that Shanshan was not aware of Jiang's marital status at the time. Thanks to the time-honored tradition of moral criticism still going strong in China, the video could cause irreparable damage before she was able to provide any explanation, which most people, more likely than not, would ignore while so absorbed in those graphic images.

And the reason why Zhonghua Petroleum Company wanted to produce such a video could not be clearer. It was intended as a devastating preemptive strike against Shanshan.

A political murder, just as the government had done with Jiang by interpreting the consultation fee as an 'environmental ransom' for the local companies. Jiang was innocent, a victim in the set-up orchestrated from above, Chen was quite sure. Still, he could not forgive Jiang for all the trouble brought to Shanshan.

Now something more sinister was being done to Shanshan, and to the people related to her. And she was still in the dark. In the event of its being posted online prior to the release of the documentary, the latter would have been doomed.

So it was up to him, as a cop as well as a man, to thwart such a devious scheme.

But how?

After listening to the tape recorded at the neighborhood office in Zabei Park, Detective Yu began debating with himself whether he should get hold of Inspector Chen to discuss the latest information and development.

Yu was now pretty sure Lou was the one. That being the case, it was the order of the day to put him into custody before his next move.

But Yu was not absolutely sure, with neither evidence nor witness.

What if he turned out to be wrong?

In that case, why should he drag the inspector into the mess?

To his surprise, a phone call came in. It was from Detective Qin.

'Anything new on your side?'

'Well, that's what I want to ask of you, Detective Qin.' Yu added deliberately, 'You have put your suspect in custody, I've heard.'

'No, not officially yet.'

'What does that mean?'

'Given the circumstances, I don't think Internal Security is one hundred percent sure about Zhou being the one. It's almost a week since Xiang's death. If nothing has happened for another week or so, then we can conclude the investigation.'

'I see.'

'Now what has your chief inspector said to you about the latest development? He's hardly been seen in the bureau for the last few days.'

'He's made a trip to Wuxi for Zhao, that's about all I know.'

Chen had mentioned his getting a phone call from Li on the Shanghai-Wuxi train, so Qin must have heard about it, too.

But Yu wondered why Qin raised the question about Chen again.

In fact, he himself did not know what Chen had been up to. If it was something about which Chen chose not to talk to him, however, it could mean that the inspector knew he was in serious trouble.

After the talk on the phone with Detective Qin, Yu dialed Chen, but without success.

In the private room of the Small River restaurant, the contents of the video began to change, shifting to scenes from another location, a startlingly different one, which immediately grabbed Inspector Chen's attention anew.

He watched on, holding his breath, as if under an inexplicable spell.

The new section of the video seemed to be of much lower resolution, rather blurred with dim light in the background. It had probably been taken in a shabby old building long out of repair.

First it presented a narrow corridor, almost like a decrepit hotel, lined with a considerable number of rooms on both sides, storing stacks of briquettes, coal stoves, piles of vegetables and other nondescript stuff outside, but otherwise a deserted corridor.

A man appeared from the landing of the stairs, heading stealthily to the middle of the corridor. What with his hat and glasses, with the poor light in the corridor, and with his moving along in a hurry, his face was practically unrecognizable.

From its angle, the hidden surveillance camera caught him looking around, groping in semi-darkness, until a shaft of light penetrating in from a cracked corridor window showed him stopping in front of a door, knocking at it uncertainly with his back to the camera.

The door opened, a young woman standing in a white terrycloth robe, barefoot and bare-legged, her hair still wet, hanging loose over her shoulders, and a soft ring of light on her face. 'Come in,' she said to the nocturnal visitor.

Recognition hit home. It was none other than Shanshan's dorm room on that long-ago night. And it was Shanshan herself reaching out her hand to the inspector, then incognito, before the door closed.

Then there was nothing else visible on the video except the deserted corridor again. The camera must have been installed somewhere opposite her door on a slight angle. It was no surprise that, for an environmental activist like Shanshan, the local government had placed a hidden camera there, as surveillance for people coming in and out of it.

So what was happening inside her dorm room was invisible to the camera. But there was no need for him to see. The scenes inside were all in his memory, like a movie he had reviewed time and again.

He pressed stop.

Remembrance was somehow self-selective on occasions. As if unwilling to be juxtaposed with the earlier scenes in the tape, he found himself focusing on what happened after their passionate moment, on his writing the poem beside her . . .

Afterward, he awoke at midnight.

She was sleeping beside him, her head nestling against his shoulder, her legs entangled with his.

Through the curtain slightly pulled aside, a shaft of moonlight peeped in, and her naked body presented a porcelain glow, a small pool of sweat beginning to dry in the hollow between her breasts, barely covered by a rumpled blanket.

So it had happened. He still found it hard to believe. It seemed as though he had been another man earlier, and was now reviewing in amazement what had happened to somebody else. He looked at her again, her black hair spilled over the white pillow, her pale face peaceful yet passion-worn, after the consummating moment of the cloud coming and the rain falling.

Again, he turned to her curled up beside him, the serene radiance of her clear features, vivid in a flood of moonlight. He was awash with gratitude.

All this was perhaps too much for him to think about for the present moment. But he had to, he told himself. To think of a plan to protect her, and then, if possible, a plan for their future.

She stirred, her shapely leg sprawling out. He could not help reaching out and tracing his fingers along her bare back, which seemed to be rippling smoothly under his touch, like the waves that begin, and ease, and then begin again, with slow, tremulous cadence.

Once again, he found himself too distracted to concentrate on the case. Nor did he want to think along that line.

So he got out, went to pick up the laptop, and moved back to the bed. Leaning back with a couple of pillows propped against the headboard, he placed the laptop above his drawn-up knees, overlooking her moon-blanched face.

He did not start all at once, sitting still, thinking, unaware of time flowing away like waves in the dark.

With her lying against him, the water of the lake made its way into that long poem, with those lines gushing out from his pen, from the lake – all through her.

Working in the attic office overlooking the eatery packed with customers, Peiqin got another short message from Lianping.

'It's announced that Zhou has been put into custody as a suspect in Xiang's murder, but the head of the newspaper also emphasized that it is not an official announcement – not to the outside.'

What did it mean?

She tried to contact Chen on the special number, but he did not pick up. He must have been so busy with the developments in his own investigation.

Her phone call to Yu was not picked up either. Getting more

worried, she was debating with herself whether she should make a visit to the police bureau. But she had delivered a basket of *Zongzi* there just the other day. Besides, she did not even know if he was in the office.

The subsequent scene in the video began. Still in the same dorm building. More than three or four hours later, according to the time recorded in the upper right corner of the image. The dorm room door suddenly opened, and she was slipping out barefoot in a large T-shirt. She was seen looking about, turning right, running toward the other end of the corridor, out of the range of the hidden camera, but in less than five minutes, hurrying back along the corridor and disappearing into the room.

The sequence of the images confused him for a second, but then he got it. Like in most factory dorm buildings, people had to share the public toilet on the same floor. She must have come out of the dorm room, light-footed, while he was still sleeping.

Again, nothing was visible on the tape for a second or two when the door closed after her, except the empty corridor.

It was about two hours later, in the grayness of the early dawn, that the door opened again. This time, it was the man coming out. With the lights out in the corridor, the visibility barely improved, and it presented a rather indistinct image of his heading toward the staircase in a hurry.

There seemed to be nothing graphic going on in that entire section, but the caption popped up:

'The adulteress spending the whole night with another secret lover in her dorm room.'

All at once, the juxtaposition of the scenes with the time recorded on them made an unequivocal impression, which the audience would most likely accept, perhaps most eagerly too.

That would deliver another devastating blow to Shanshan.

He pressed stop on the video, tapping his fingers on the table.

The camera must have been installed with the governmental instruction then.

So was the government now ordering the making of the video from Rong?

According to Rong, however, it was a state-run company that had given the job to an outsider like him.

Whoever was behind the making of the video must have been able to secure some of the contents from the government, and for a mega state-run company like Zhonghua Petroleum Company, it made sense.

Still sitting on a bench in Zabei Park, Detective Yu found a text message from Peiqin on his phone. It could have come in while he was busy listening to the tape. It was about the message from Lianping to Peiqin.

Yu was not exactly surprised at Lianping's going out of her way to help. He now saw clearly it was because of Inspector Chen, after what Peiqin had said to him the other night.

But for the moment, he had to focus on the development in the investigation. Internal Security and Detective Qin were moving fast to their conclusion. Once officially declared, there was no turning over the table.

What else could Yu possibly do?

With its door closed, the private room in Small River was getting hot as Chen moved to click the start button again for the video.

The next part consisted of scenes at different locations, in sharp contrast to the previous one.

In this new section, Shanshan was seen moving gracefully in upper-class society, with pictures of her stepping out of a brand new Mercedes, entering into a grand villa with an immense meadow surrounding it, carrying a Hermès purse at a private airport, lying immersed in the bubbles of a Jacuzzi tub and holding a glass of champagne in her slender hand, like a toast to an invisible man holding the camera.

In the midst of all these, the intimate scenes of her with Yao in the moments of 'cloud and rain' were interspersed.

In the second century BC, Song Yu, a celebrated poet of the Chu State, composed a rhapsody about the liaison of King Xiang of Chu and the Goddess of the Wu Mountains. Parting after a passionate night, the glamorous goddess promised she would come again and again to him in 'clouds and rain', which had since turned into a breathtaking metaphor for sexual love in classical Chinese literature.

Thousands of years later, the scenes of rolling cloud and pouring rain were sweeping over the laptop screen under Chen's gaze, just like in the ancient rhapsody:

> *I live in the high mountains south of Wu, turning into colorful cloud in the morning, and into misting drizzle in the evening, day and night, turning into all the shapes and forms of your lord's imagination . . .*

Was it just happening in the ancient rhapsody, or through it, in his mind's eye?

After the previous two sections, these scenes came as no real shock to the inspector, as if in sequence of the same theme, but at different locations.

A caption crept up underneath: 'A soulless gold digger in the disguise of a public intellectual, who ensnared a rich businessman back from the United States – all for the sake of his money.'

Some of the pictures seemed to be of excellent quality, Chen noted, with her properly posed in good lighting and photographed in high resolution, unlike the product of a hidden camera. The pictures of the moment of 'cloud and rain' appeared revealing, but at the same time not too revealing, sensual but not erotic. They could have been taken by Yao with some selfie instruments, and then stolen from his computer.

Combined with the previous sections, however, it would inevitably give rise to the impression of a light or even promiscuous woman, particularly with another caption shooting up: 'Look at the date on the images. She moved in with him long before their marriage.'

Prenuptial affairs were no big deal in today's China, especially for those who got married afterward, but given the context, it reinforced the earlier message about her being one of easy virtue, at least in the eyes of the implied viewers.

He pressed stop again.

The video was reaching its end. He did not have to continue watching, though he had not yet seen anything in her own words from the hacked emails, which were probably still being hacked or edited.

It was a no-brainer to figure out that the video was being made to annihilate Shanshan – along with her documentary. It was like an ancient proverb: 'To stop cooking, it is the most effective to pull all the firewood out of the stove.'

Chen thought he could guess who had ordered the making of the video.

Kang, the head of Zhonghua Petroleum Company, having heard of the documentary in the making, was worried about the interview with Shanshan at the time when the GDP-justifying-everything arrogance had been seen as politically correct, in line with the official propaganda about economic development being the one and only truth at whatever expense. But things were turning out to be quite different now. The environmental expense was too huge, and his argument would have infuriated the mask-wearing viewers. What's more, the documentary had gathered so much irrefutable evidence about the company riding roughshod over environmental regulations, and causing horrible damage to the people's health. With the public outcry louder than ever in the air pollution crisis, and with the man behind the 'petroleum gang' losing in the power struggle, Kang could be conveniently thrown out as a scapegoat, so he must have been desperate to prevent the release of the documentary.

In *The Thirty-Six Stratagems,* one of the stratagems was 'to rescue the State of Zhao by attacking the State of Wei'. In a devious attempt to save his neck, Kang had secretly ordered the making of the tape, by hook or by crook, against Shanshan.

But that was a game two could play.

A knock was heard on the door.

Instead of sending Inspector Chen the text message about Lou's jogging in the early morning, and about the interview at the neighborhood committee, Detective Yu decided to do one more thing since he was in the neighborhood.

The neighborhood committee had been a dynamic 'watchdog' for the Party authorities during the Mao period, when the word *yinsi* – privacy – did not exactly exist in the Chinese language. If anything, *yinsi* was totally negative, meaning something done in secret from the surveillance of the 'revolutionary people'. So the committee could have done everything in those years in the name of the 'class struggle', spying on and suspecting anyone as a possible 'class enemy'. In recent years, however, it was no longer that easy for a committee member to barge into a resident's home without a justifiable reason.

Yu left the park. It took him less than ten minutes to get back to the apartment building, of which Lou's was on the sixth floor. For an apartment without an elevator, it required some energy to climb to the top floor, but it was the least expensive in the building.

On the sixth floor, the door to Lou's unit was locked, as was no surprise, and Yu knocked on the door opposite.

It opened with a slender woman in her mid-thirties reaching out wearing her florid pajamas, barefoot in plastic slippers.

Yu raised a finger to his lips and handed over his police badge to her.

Examining the badge, she nodded and let him into her apartment without much ado.

'My name is Mi,' she said, gesturing for him to sit on an old leather-covered chair in a scantily furnished room. She had a lean face and pale, thin lips.

'I just want to ask some questions about your neighbor, Lou. And I hope I won't take too much of your time.'

'Ask any questions you want to ask. I got fired from my old job last month, and I am still looking for a new one. Time is one thing I have a lot of nowadays. Did he do something horrible?'

'We don't really know anything yet. But perhaps you can help by telling me about what you know about him?'

'He moved in here only half a year or so ago, but prior to that, he and Shen, still his girlfriend at the time, came quite regularly to renovate the apartment opposite, doing all the hard work themselves. Not well-to-do, but a loving, happy young couple they were! But about a month after they moved in, she was checked into the hospital. What a tragic story! You must have heard about it.'

'He must have been so devastated.'

'Yes, he's a totally different man after her death.'

'So is there anything strange, abnormal about him now?'

'It's difficult for one to remain normal after suffering such a terrible loss. From time to time, he could be heard weeping alone in the apartment. And cursing too.'

'So he shut himself up all the time?'

'Not all the time, but he could stay in for the whole day.'

'He does not go to work any more?'

'I think he took his leave, but you may have to ask his company about it,' she said, wetting her lips with the tip of her tongue. 'And there may be something else. He spares no expense for the seven-seven ritual for her at home, you know, bringing basketfuls of fish and meat for the meal dedicated to her every week. Now it is conventional to invite other family members to the seven-seven meal, for he surely buys enough for a "round table banquet". But you know what? He declared he just wanted to be with her alone. No relatives or friends were invited. He simply locked himself in with her tablet on the table. And almost all the food was dumped afterward.'

'He's beside himself with grief.'

'But believe it or not, he may be already trying to get back on his feet.'

'What do you mean, Mi?'

'Shortly after her death – a week or so – he started jogging in the morning.'

'Jogging regularly?'

'No, not regularly. Perhaps once or twice a week. He gets up earlier than almost all the people in the building. I have slept badly lately, waking up around three or four, you know, since I lost my job. So I heard him walking down early several times. I looked out the window and saw him jogging.'

'But what's strange about that, Mi?'

'Lou's so heartbroken. How could he have had the heart to jog out early in the morning?'

'That might just be his way of dealing with sadness. You can never tell.'

'And there's something else. About a week ago, with his door ajar, I happened to overhear Lou talking to a real estate agent and a buyer about selling off the apartment. It's understandable that he wants to get out of the place with everything there reminding him of her, but where is he going to stay?'

'Back with his parents, probably.'

'But he never will be able to buy another one for himself. He borrowed a lot of money for her treatment in the hospital, we all know. It's about a month after she left, and he has not gone back to work. And now he's selling the apartment.'

'Yes, *like there's no tomorrow for him*, that's what a neighborhood committee member told me. Anything else?'

'I think I've told you everything. Having said all that, I want to add that things may not be strange or suspicious at all, considering his circumstances. We should not be too hard on such a grief-stricken man, Detective Yu.'

'I cannot agree more. Thank you so much, Mi. Here is my business card. If you think of anything else, let me know.'

Lou's door remained shut. Yu moved downstairs.

Halfway down the stairs, an idea tumbled across his mind. The selling of Lou's apartment through a real estate agent. The third victim, Yan, was an agent in Zabei District. But then he ruled out the possibility. Yan was killed in Lujiazui, Pudong, and according to Mi, Lou was with the agent here just a week ago. So it could be anybody but her.

Standing up, Chen pulled out the memory stick and closed the laptop before moving to open the private room's door.

The light pouring in from outside disoriented him for a moment. He blinked in confusion upon seeing a figure. It was Melong standing there.

Like in an ancient Chinese saying: 'Seven days high in a mountain cave, and a thousand years down in the mundane world.'

The inspector had spent perhaps less than an hour watching the video in the private room, but it appeared as if he had lived a large part of his life moving back and forth in the midst of these fast-shifting scenes.

'So what do you think, Chief?'

The return of Melong derailed the train of his thoughts. Chen was at a momentary loss for words. No point discussing the contents of the video with Melong, who might have already viewed it – or at least part of it. And he could have recognized the man moving in and out of Shanshan's room in the video. That explained Melong's stepping out earlier, to make 'business phone calls', so the inspector could watch all by himself.

'Can Rong try to do anything about the video?' Chen said as soon as Melong closed the door after him.

'What do you want him to do, Chief Inspector Chen? I may have put him off turning in the video to his client, I suppose, for a couple of days, but probably not longer than that, I'm afraid. It's a sizable sum of money for him, and his client will not let him put it off for too long.'

'The video does not look properly edited yet. Has his client viewed it as it is?'

'No, I don't think so.'

'In that case, could Rong tell them that he's unable to deliver in time? For one reason or another – for whatever reason – it's undeliverable for a couple of weeks. Let him claim that the tape got accidentally wiped out and he has to start all over.'

'I don't think his client will like it. Rong has to worry about more than the loss of money. The client may choose to scrap the video project for him.'

'Well, as for his possible loss, I think I may work out an adequate compensation. Better than his client's pay. Say three hundred thousand yuan. Don't worry about the sum. I'll have it reimbursed through the Party Central Discipline Committee in Beijing.'

The last sentence was partially true. At least as far as Zhao had promised him. For that amount a lot of questions would have to be asked, and he did not think he wanted to answer any of them. For now, it was just something said for the benefit of Melong, and Rong, too. For the imperative impression that Chief Inspector Chen was not acting alone, crazily, like Don Quixote fighting the gigantic windmill.

Melong did not make an immediate response.

'Five or sixty thousand yuan here, I believe,' Chen said, snapping out a credit card. 'And I'll go to the bank this afternoon. And to some Big Buck friends, too. The total sum shall be available tomorrow evening.'

'Don't worry too much about the money. I too have some cash at home,' Melong said. 'You keep the memory stick. I'll go to Rong's place right now. I don't know if he will agree with the plan. I have to talk to him in person.'

Inspector Chen parted with Melong outside the restaurant, but he made no more than seven or eight steps when Melong turned round and caught up with him.

'Something else, Chief. I almost forgot.'

'Go ahead, Melong.'

'About the video, not the one I showed you today but the one going viral online. Someone purchased it from the club.'

'It's unbelievable. The club must have been aware who Geng is in the Party system.'

'Yes, but for a club like this, the people there have to keep some cards in hand. You can never tell what might happen to them one of these days.'

'So it's like a bargaining chip?'

'Yes. Now Geng's reaching his retirement age, and soon the younger ones will be coming into power. Things might be really complicated with the power struggle going on not only here but in the Forbidden City, too. Of course, some buyer could have offered an unbelievable price, and the club people could not say no.'

'An offer he can't refuse, like in *The Godfather*. Now just one more question. Do you have any idea when it was purchased?'

'About a couple of years ago. But why?'

'I don't know yet.'

After parting again with Melong, it occurred to Inspector Chen that he had not had a bite since last evening.

The turtle mentioned in Melong's message had just been a pretext, but it might be as well for him to skip a meal or two. The sensation of the steamed turtle the previous day still stayed heavy on his empty stomach.

He decided to walk by himself for a short while.

Then he realized something else. Far more worrisome than the monstrous turtle or the empty stomach.

With the video not yet edited into a viewable one, whoever had given the order must still have a copy of the original contents in their possession, including the pictures hacked from Shanshan's computer or her husband's, and the scenes recorded in the surveillance cameras. In the event of Rong's failure to deliver, they just needed another man for the job.

It was a matter of time before Kang would try to turn the tables by releasing it earlier than Shanshan's documentary.

What could the tourist guide/inspector possibly do?

He took out a rumpled pack of China, shaking out the last cigarette left in it. In a desperate need for nicotine, he lit it, pledging that it would be the last one for him, provided he could find a way – any way – to keep her from harm.

A terrible fit of coughing seized him again at the first two or three inhales, to the disgust of a young couple walking by, wearing large masks, holding each other's hand.

All is justifiable in love and war.

When he looked up again, he caught sight of another restaurant across the street – Fishing in the Muddled Water.

The restaurant name, apparently highlighting fish as its chef's special, was logical since the restaurants here were known for the sea- or river-food. Coincidentally, the name also came from *The Thirty-Six Stratagems*, in which 'fishing in the muddled water' is listed as the number twenty stratagem. When used for a restaurant name, it carried a touch of post-modernist irony.

As if reeling in a murky stream of consciousness, he thought of Kang's video again. There was nothing the inspector could do – not until the situation got muddled up; only then an opportunity for him to catch fish in confusion.

He crushed the cigarette underfoot, pulled out the phone and called Zhao, still having a bit of a coughing fit.

'I was thinking of calling you too, Chen. Are you coming down with a cold or something?'

'No, it's just because of the smog irritation. Don't worry about it, Comrade Secretary Zhao.'

'Well, first let me ask you a question about your last

message,' Zhao came straight to the point. 'What do you mean by yourself being followed?'

'The day after I talked to you in the hotel, I went to see Qiang, the head of the foreign liaison office in the Shanghai Writers' Association. As your designated tourist guide, I needed suggestions about what a visitor may find interesting in the city – that's what Qiang's office usually does for visiting foreign writers. But about half an hour after our talk in the café that afternoon, he disappeared. And there's still no trace or news whatsoever about him, even today. I cannot but wonder if his disappearance could have had something to do with my talk to him.'

'Did you tell him I'm on vacation in Shanghai?'

'No, he had heard of your visit to Shanghai through his own channels. He's said to be a secret officer of Internal Security. But I talked to him only about the air quality at the local tourist attractions. It's crucial for a fresh air vacation.'

'Any other specific questions he asked of you?'

'I remember he asked me whether you're concerned with the air pollution, and with people's complaining about it. He recommended me a new product called "Fresh Canadian Air". It comes in an aluminum can made in Canada, which you may carry around and breathe in whenever and wherever needed. Usable for about one thousand inhales, but still quite expensive.'

What he was telling Zhao was mostly true. Like a lot of things in this world, however, whether something's true or not really depends on the interpretation, and on the perspective one chooses.

'Well, that can be something, I mean Qiang's disappearance.'

'I'm nobody, Comrade Secretary Zhao. I don't see why they would have invited "somebody out for a cup of tea" simply because of a talk he had with me. For a more likely scenario, some people must have been suspicious of the investigation I've been doing for you, and detained Qiang at an unknown location for questioning.'

'You're being way too modest about yourself, Comrade Chief Inspector Chen, but it won't hurt for you to be careful.'

That at least was not a downright no. The scenario proved

not to be that unimaginable to Zhao. The inspector said nothing more, waiting for the theory to sink in.

'Now what have you done with your report?' Zhao changed the subject abruptly. 'I need something with more solid details.'

'I'm working on it. It's quite a long and detailed report, that much I can assure you. Hopefully I'll deliver it to you in a day or two.'

It was a self-imposed deadline, which he needed more urgently in the light of the latest information from the restaurant. He touched the flash memory stick in his pocket.

'Good. I'm looking forward to reading it.'

When Detective Yu got back home that evening, it was past nine.

Peiqin was on their bed, reading a magazine with a pair of new glasses under the lamp.

'Another busy day for you, I bet.'

Last night they had had a long discussion about the serial murder case, so Peiqin was looking forward to learning something new.

'Yes, another lousy day.'

'I'll warm up the fried noodles with organic spinach. The purple seaweed soup will take just a minute or two on the stove.'

'Don't bother. I've had a bite on the way back. But a cup of tea may help.' He added, 'I think I've a lot to discuss with you.'

'That's fine, a cup of your favorite Uloon will be ready in one minute,' Peiqin said, jumping barefoot from the bed. 'Still about that serial murder case of yours?'

Sipping at the tea, Yu began to tell her what had happened during the day: about his following Lou to the New World in the morning, about the investigation done concerning Lou in his neighborhood, and about the bits and pieces from Lou's company which Yu visited after the neighborhood committee, including some of the latest information he had not even discussed with Chen yet.

Like him, like Chen, Peiqin had little doubt about Lou being the one, but she maintained that Yu should discuss it with Qin and his people before attempting to do anything.

'After all, it's their case, and they have everything at their disposal for any action they want to take. And for any responsibility, too.'

Peiqin surely had a point, but she knew little about the politics in the bureaus. He did not think that Qin would listen to him. Not at this moment.

The sex video about Geng and Xiang must have so convinced Qin and Internal Security of the political direction they had been pursuing.

In contrast, Yu had nothing except an unlikely theory supported with neither evidence nor witnesses.

And he would have too much explaining to do about how he had come along to this point – with no cooperation with Qin's squad.

Instead, Yu chose to talk more about the seven-seven ritual with Peiqin.

'Lou's such a grief-distraught husband,' Peiqin said softly in response. 'It's not unimaginable that the sight of the caregiver walking out of the hospital – at that place, at that minute – triggered the killing. For the seven-seven ritual or not, he must have seen some real justification for the killings in his twisted mind.'

'I think you're right about that. Supposing he turned murderous on the spur of that moment, at that place – what about the other victims?'

'His wife died of lung cancer, and people have been complaining about the polluted air as the cause of the disease. For such a long time, our weather bureau kept saying the air's perfectly fine—'

'Hold on, Detective Peiqin. That may really throw some light on the choice of his second victim in the People's Square – the weather anchorman Linghu,' Yu said, sitting up. 'Still, what about the third and fourth victims?'

'I don't know, but people are angry about so many things, though the anchorman should not have been held personally responsible for it.'

'It's a brilliant point, I'll discuss it with Chen. A solid connection there.'

'So what else are you going to do?'

'I don't know,' he said, guessing Peiqin would start arguing against what he planned to do the next morning. 'I've not decided yet. After such a long day, I'm really beaten. I think I'll sleep on it.'

But he was sure he would get up early again the next morning.

DAY FIVE
FRIDAY

Inspector Chen looked up from the computer to the clock on the wall. It was already past midnight. The silence of the apartment was intense.

He had tried to doze for a while with the printout of the incomplete report lying aside on the desk, but he was unable to do so.

It would probably make more sense for him to deliver the report to Zhao in a long, detailed email, rather than in person. He was not sure whether Zhao, sitting opposite with all the political seriousness imaginable, would permit him to say what he wanted to without stopping him after a few sentences.

For a senior Party leader like Zhao, he had to make the Party's interests his first priority. No matter how Chen might try to spin the documentary, it would be a nearly impossible mission to win Zhao over with nothing but an objective report.

Still, the inspector had to make the attempt. After all, there are interpretations and *interpretations* of the Party's interests.

He forced himself to sit down and begin writing.

> I'm writing this report to you because it's been such an unusual investigation, Comrade Secretary Zhao, with the complications unexpected and some of them unimaginable to me.
>
> As I've mentioned, I managed to sneak into a meeting at the New World with Yuan Jing and her associates there without being recognized. An important part of the meeting was for a preview of a documentary in the making. I wasn't able to get a copy of it, but afterward I double-checked and researched some of the things

represented in it. It took me quite a while to do so, and
what I can put in the report today may still not be
detailed enough. For a general impression, however, it is
a well-done and researched documentary and, at the
same time, with the combination of texts and images, it
is also easily understandable and acceptable to the broad
mass of people.

The air pollution is such a serious problem for our
country, as you have told me, and we have to deal with
it in different ways, at different levels. One of the effective
ways is to raise people's awareness of the environmental
crisis through a basic understanding of the causes. The
documentary could be truly educational and enlightening
for that purpose.

I, for one, have learned such a lot from it.

At this stage, I cannot tell what the documentary
will eventually look like when completed. It could take
a couple of weeks for them to finish it. And then, probably an even longer process of their submitting it to
the censorship office for the approval of its eventual
release.

For the battle against air pollution, it is imperative for
our Party to lead the people, and I believe the release
of the documentary under governmental guidance will
demonstrate our Party's determination to fight on the
side of the people . . .

He moved on to a more detailed analysis, arguing that most of
the points raised in Shanshan's documentary would prove to
be thought-provoking, not only to the ordinary people, but
to the government officials too, as the mounting public outcry
about the horrendous air quality could be seen as something
threatening the legitimacy of the Party rule. As for some politically sensitive material in the documentary, he maintained that
the censorship office would effectively take care of it, so there
was no possibility of the documentary coming into conflict
with the Party's interests.

In the middle of all of this, he did not mention Shanshan's
plan to post it online instead of submitting it for approval of

its release. Anyway, that was not something discussed in the meeting at the club in the New World.

Then came a crucial part in his report. Judging by Zhao's earlier response to the info regarding Zhonghua Petroleum Company and Qiang's disappearance, it might not be such a long shot to assume some conspiracies going on high up, even involving senior leaders like Zhao at the top.

As there are interpretations and *interpretations* about things working in the Party's interest or against it, it was not unimaginable for Zhao to see any attempt against him as against the Party's interests, though the other factions opposing him in the Forbidden City saw it the other way around.

Hence the possibility for Chen to apply the stratagem of 'killing a man with another man's knife', as explored in that ancient classic Zhao had also read.

Chen continued his report.

In the course of the investigation, I've been more and more concerned with some Party cadres' attitude toward the environmental crisis. One concrete example in the documentary is Yuan Jing's interview with Kang of Zhonghua Petroleum Company. His argument is simply so GDP-oriented, careless of ecological consequences, and callous to people's suffering. With the release of the documentary, we will convince our people that we're opposing such practices as represented by Kang, making serious efforts to combat it and taking their interests to heart. So I'm enclosing a copy of the entire interview between Kang and Yuan Jing.

And during the investigation, I also noticed something else highly suspicious and disturbing. Qiang's mysterious disappearance, which I have already briefed you about earlier. It's a horror to think that they're aware I've been doing the job for you – under your personal instruction – but they still went ahead like that. With clues and evidence still coming in, I think I'll have to make a personal report to you about it in a couple of days. It could have been orchestrated by somebody higher

above, with real power, and perhaps with Internal
Security at his control, too.

These were shots in the dark, which Chen had to fire.

Those who backed the petroleum group behind the scenes,
as whispered, had been involved in some power struggle at
the top. If this was the case, how would Zhao have reacted?

It was worth trying to have Zhao do or not do something
in his own interest, something that could have a bearing on
the release of the documentary at the same time, otherwise
Zhao would most likely go ahead and have the documentary
nipped in the bud.

Perhaps there was not much more Chen could put into the
report, but he nonetheless added a couple of sentences toward
the end.

> In the meantime, I've been trying to get a copy of the
> documentary for you, so you may make the call.
> She's still editing it, and it'll take a couple of weeks
> before its release. So we have the time to look further
> into it.

It was not likely that the report would appeal to a senior Party
leader like Zhao in the normal circumstances. Under the
present circumstances, however, Inspector Chen thought he
still had a slight chance. It might work. It might backfire, too.
It was a high-stakes gamble.

He had to turn the report in today, though he was still not
satisfied with it.

Finally, as Chen typed out his name at the end of the report,
it was almost five in the morning.

The bridge was burnt, the boat was sunk, and there was no
retreating.

But he did not click send. The first gray of the morning
was already beginning to filter into the room as he got up
from the desk.

There was no point going to bed now. He moved to the
microwave, rewarmed a cup of coffee left overnight, and
finished it in two gulps.

He thought about sending a text message to Yu, but decided against it. It was too early.

Putting a copy of the magazine into a large envelope, he was ready to set out.

Detective Yu woke up with a startle, breaking into a cold sweat.

Peiqin was sleeping beside him, one of her bare legs placed across his on the blanket, just like in their 'educated youth' days. She had hardly changed, at least not in this aspect.

But Yu did not fall back to sleep until past three, blinking at some patterns shifting across the ceiling, like crouching monsters in the shadows.

Now he was wide awake again, having closed his eyes for less than an hour.

It was the day that the murderer would most likely strike out again.

Yu sat up, placed Peiqin's leg lightly on the bed, and got down on his tiptoes.

For Detective Yu, Friday morning in front of Lou's apartment building in Zabei was pretty much a repetition of Thursday morning, except that it started earlier with his stationing himself behind a flowering apple tree.

If today was the day, Lou had to come out to reach the New World for the action before six – in accordance with the established time pattern.

At ten to five, with the sky still so smoggy and somber, Yu saw Lou stepping out, breaking into a jog for a block before slowing down and turning to the direction of the subway station.

Like the previous day, Yu followed him across a couple of blocks and into the station. It was five, the exact time for the first subway train.

It was all Yu could do to get into the same train without being detected. Fortunately, there were already so many passengers, even at that early hour.

Holding on to the railing ring hung from above, Yu was pretty sure about the destination of the subway trip: the New World.

Sure enough, after changing to another train on Line 10, Lou got out at the New World.

Inspector Chen found himself in Bund Park again.

Standing on the bank near the park entrance, he glanced up at the big clock atop the Custom House Building. It was still too early for him to assume the role of an inspector on a secret mission.

Instead, he started strolling about the park in unhurried steps, like years earlier, trying to clear his mind in the fresh morning air.

Except that it was anything but the fresh morning air of the past.

He mounted a flight of steps to the color-stone promenade overlooking the river. A petrel seemed to come out of nowhere, gliding over the murky waves, its wings flashing in the somber gray light.

Perhaps it was soaring out of a half-forgotten dream.

In the early seventies, as a 'waiting-for-assignment-middle-school-graduate' caught in the national campaign launched by Mao, of 'the educated youths going to the countryside for the re-education from the poor and lower-middle class peasants', Chen was left waiting in the city for recovery from his bronchitis, out of school, out of a job. Along with several neighbors, he came to practice tai chi in Bund Park, but on one mist-enveloped morning, after yet another half-hearted attempt at copying those ancient tai chi poses, he realized it wasn't for him.

Instead, he decided to bring to the park with him an old English textbook and sit on a bench. Those days, few would have carried such a book – except as a placemat for the dew-drenched bench. It became the first link in a long, long chain of causality for him. In the park, he began his English studies, which opened up a brave new world.

In retrospect, life seemed to be so full of the *ironical causalities of misplaced Yin and Yang*, like the misplaced book in that park, like the misplaced youth in those years, or like the misplaced chief inspector today. One thing led to another, and to still another . . .

Then he moved down, looking for a bench. That green-painted bench, once his customary seat in the park, was long gone, though he still remembered a slogan carved on its back: *Long Live the Proletarian Dictatorship.*

Behind Chen, an elderly man in a white silk martial art costume, loose-sleeved, red-silk buttoned, started practicing tai chi by himself, wearing such a peaceful expression on his face, and an electronic filtered mask over his mouth, which made him look more like a robot in a sci-fi movie, striking out one graceful, time-honored pose after another: *grasping a bird's tail, spreading a white crane's wings, parting a wild horse's mane on both sides . . .* Chen watched him pushing out the right hand, and then the left hand, as if fighting against the invisible particles in the contaminated air.

Unable to find a bench in the too-much-changed park, he seated himself instead on the stone step close to the north entrance. He wanted to read the poem one more time.

Once in the New World, Lou started jogging again, circling the area and looking around.

It was another smoggy morning, and it was not easy for Lou to note that he was being followed.

And for the same reason, it was not easy for the target to discover that he or she was being followed.

Lou was catching up with a middle-aged woman walking in front.

What was Detective Yu going to do?

Under the normal circumstances, Yu would have been able to fall back on Chen, and in some cases, on other colleagues because of Chen. However idiosyncratic Chen appeared to others in the bureau, his opinions carried weight, with a number of major cases to his credit.

So Detective Yu could have said to others in the bureau, 'That's the opinion of Chief Inspector Chen.' And they might have chosen to work together with him.

Not this time, though.

Chen had to remain officially off the case. And Yu's opinion could hardly have mattered.

But this morning, the seventh morning after the appearance

of Xiang's body near the *Wenhui* building, could be the very day for Lou to act. The crucial seventh day in the weekly cycle. There was little possibility of Lou's putting it off to another day.

So it was also the day for Detective Yu to act.

For him, the question was how.

Could he choose to wait until the moment Lou took out the weapon – most likely the hammer – to stop the murderer?

Given the distance between Lou and the target, was Detective Yu capable of preventing the crime in time?

With no help or backup whatsoever, he was not sure that he would be able to arrest Lou single-handedly.

And even if Lou was apprehended there, another lost life could have been added to the casualty list of the serial murderer. 'I can never forgive myself,' he vividly recalled Inspector Chen saying with a ghastly pale face after failing to save an innocent victim.

Alternatively, Detective Yu could choose to act preemptively, before another victim was claimed under the smoggy morning sky.

The seven-seven scenario could turn out, however, to be a false one.

To have an innocent man arrested in the open at the New World, Yu knew, would prove to be too much of a public embarrassment to the bureau, particularly at this sensitive juncture, especially under the circumstances of his making the move without having discussed it with the bureau, and as a result his days as a cop would be numbered.

Nevertheless, Yu moved closer behind Lou, who seemed to be doing the same to the middle-aged woman.

It was five forty. Not too much time left according to the time pattern for Lou.

It turned out, however, to be a false alarm, as the woman turned into a small alley in the New World and stepped into the first *shikumen* house with the black-painted door already open. Perhaps she worked there – a Cantonese restaurant inside the *shikumen*.

For a couple of times in the next several minutes, Lou closed in on other people – apparently at a striking distance.

Detective Yu became increasingly doubtful about his being able to move up in time to stop Lou – Lou could flash out his hammer in a split second.

Yu sweated profusely. He noticed for the first time that Lou's trouser pocket was slightly bulging. He quickened his steps, moving to a closer distance behind Lou, almost bumping against him.

It was a call for Detective Yu to make. No more than five minutes to six. Lou was now closing fast on a white-haired man close to La Maison, suddenly plunging his hand into his pocket . . .

As Inspector Chen opened the magazine in the park, a cool breeze was carrying a melody over from the big clock atop the Shanghai Customs Building. Six o'clock. It had been one of the 'reddest tunes', *The East Is Red*, in praise of Mao as a great savior of China during the Cultural Revolution. After the ending of the Cultural Revolution in 1976, a light-hearted tune took its place, but now once again it was *The East Is Red* being played over the Bund.

As if on cue, loud music was coming out of a small square in the park. It was something new in the city, commonly called 'square dancing' or 'old aunties' dancing'. A huge hit among old people, who threw themselves into a sort of dance/exercise wherever they could find any open space as a temporary stage, with CD players blaring the music around.

Chen saw nothing wrong with it, but it happened to be another 'red song' popular during the Cultural Revolution. Perhaps the old people were just being reminiscent of their youthful days.

There was no stepping back twice into the same park.

He found it hard to concentrate on the poem, but he did not really have to. Those lines were inerasable images in his mind. Still, he needed the feeling of sitting there in the park, thinking, and holding the magazine in his hand.

The visit to the park would help, hopefully, to regroup his mind, just like in the mornings so many years earlier, or like Antaeus's effort to regain his strength by coming into contact with the earth.

During those long-ago mornings here, he had made for himself a number of future plans, none of which came close to what was happening to him on this gray, smoggy morning.

Looking over his shoulder, he could hardly discern the silhouette of the Hyatt Hotel across the river.

As he was about to leave the park, his cellphone started ringing.

So early in the morning. He thought he could guess who was calling, and he hurried into a recess behind a small bamboo groove in the park and picked up the phone.

'I've got him, Chief.'

'You've got Lou, Detective Yu?'

'Yes.'

'Where?'

'The New World.'

'The New World!'

'Not far from the café where we met just the day before, under the poster of those French bong bong dancers.'

'Near La Maison. I'll be damned. Another central location indeed.'

'And it's pretty much like you have suspected.'

Detective Yu moved on with a hurried account of what had happened there earlier that morning, though some of the details seemed vague, particularly about how he had managed to forestall Lou's move.

'Did Lou put up a fight?'

'Not really, but he insists he was just jogging here in the morning – jogging in the New World after taking two subway trains indeed.'

'Where are you now, Yu?'

'In a backroom of the Zhapu Neighborhood Police Station.'

'That's not far from the park on the Bund, right?'

'That's right. I happened to know a young cop named Teng at the station. He's letting me keep Lou there temporarily, but Lou is refusing to say anything. So what shall we do now?'

'You stopped him before he lashed out in the New World?'

'Yes, it was too much of a risk. He moved so dangerously close to a white-haired man walking in front of him, plunging his hand into his pocket. Sure enough, he had a hammer hidden there.'

'He must have cleaned the hammer thoroughly?'

'I think so too. No blood or anything on it. But we can send it to the lab.'

'You had to stop him before his delivering the blow. I too would have done so; best to stop a would-be-attempted crime, even with no witnesses or evidence.' Chen went on without waiting for a response, 'What did he say about the hammer?'

'He said that after jogging, he was going to his old home for some odd jobs. It does not make any sense for him to jog along carrying a heavy hammer in his pocket.'

'No, no sense at all.'

'But he refused to say anything else with such a vacant look in his bloodshot eyes. Oh, when I first got hold of him, he murmured, "Just three more".'

'With three more victims, he would be able to complete the seven-seven rituals. That's what he meant.'

'Yes, I think so too. But I cannot take him back to the bureau right now. Imagine how Qin would react to the dramatic turn.'

'You mean you have not told Detective Qin or Party Secretary Li about your work on Lou?'

'No, not anything. I tried to talk to Qin, you know, about your point regarding the inexplicable presence of the masks in the crime scenes, but he hardly listened to a sentence before brushing it off as irrelevant. Our squad's supposed to serve merely as consultant, and he's unwilling to take us seriously, especially when he believes he himself is on the right track.'

'So pushing the murderer in front of him, out of the blue, you're literally pulling the carpet from under his feet. It's difficult to tell how he would react to the surprising turn.'

'Exactly. Detective Qin would take me as withholding the information from him. So would Party Secretary Li. But I cannot keep Lou here for too long, a couple of hours, maybe, but no more than that. Soon the bureau people will come to know about it one way or another.'

'That may be true, but you may go ahead and tell them that it has been my idea for you to investigate in secret. You have discussed it with me every step of the way, and this morning it was also my direct order for you to take the preemptive move. As the head of our squad, I'm the one responsible for it.'

'No, I cannot do so, Chief Inspector Chen.'

'Don't worry about it. Tell them I have been moving in accordance with Comrade Secretary Zhao's specific instructions.'

That was far-fetched, Chen knew, but he did not think Party Secretary Li would go so far as to double-check with Comrade Secretary Zhao, especially when Lou proved to be the murderer.

And Chen also felt justified in saying so. As Zhao had put it, things have to be seen in a larger picture. With the environmental crisis seen as one threatening the legitimacy of one-Party rule, the speedy arrest of the serial murderer was more than justified.

That did not sound so convincing, even to the inspector himself. And he knew Yu would not let him take responsibility.

'And out of spite, Qin may actually choose to let Lou go if he continues to deny it.'

'And then Lou will stop at nothing to complete the killings – until the end of the seventh week.'

'Where are you, Chief?'

'Bund Park.'

'Your feng shui place again.'

People had joked about it, but in a way, it was a feng shui place for Chen. He had started his studies here, and what happened afterward could be traced to the park.

Twenty years gone,
it's a surprise I'm still here.

The lines from the Song dynasty poem forced their way back to him again. It was more than twenty years. A blue jay flashed through the opaque morning air. Inspector Chen made up his mind.

It was perhaps no coincidence: he was making another crucial decision in the park.

'Return to the backroom, Yu. Make sure that there's just Lou and you in there.'

'You want. . .' Yu did not go on with the rest of the sentence.

'Yes, then what?'

'Put your cellphone speaker on. I'll call in and say something to Lou. A conference call, so to speak.'

Two minutes later, Yu dialed Chen again.

'OK, it's on speaker now,' Yu said. Then turning to Lou, 'On the speaker now is Chief Inspector Chen, the head of the Special Case squad of the Shanghai Police Bureau.'

'Hi Lou, my name is Chen Cao. Let me be clear about one thing first: I'm not in charge of the investigation of your case. It's because I've been doing another investigation about an environmental activist for the Party Central Discipline Committee, alongside which I'm not supposed to be doing any other cases. So whatever we are talking about on the phone is off the record. You don't have to worry about it.'

'Yes?'

'You do not know me, but I know your story, which my partner Detective Yu has told me in great detail. It's a heart-breaking story, I have to say. My deepest condolences—'

'I've heard of you, Chief Inspector Chen. You may not be a bad cop. And according to my late wife, who read your poems, you may not be a bad writer, either. Still, you don't have to waste your time with me. I'm innocent, as I've told Detective Yu. I won't say anything else. It's far more important for you to concentrate on the investigation against the environmental activist.'

'Coincidentally, the activist named Shanshan is making a documentary about the disastrous air pollution in China. It is truly an important, meaningful project – whatever investigation my boss in Beijing may want me to do – and I pledge myself to keep any harm from happening to her. On the contrary, I will ensure the eventual release of her documentary.'

It was the first time Yu had learned anything about Chen's investigation under Zhao. The way Chen spoke about it reminded Yu of something Peiqin had told him, the romantic experience of the poet inspector in Wuxi, but it was not a moment for his thoughts to wander away from the present case, Detective Yu hastened to tell himself.

'You really mean that, Chief Inspector Chen?' Lou said, looking up with a sudden light in his eyes, as if Chen had been sitting opposite him across the desk.

'Yes, I give you my word, Lou.'

'Chief Inspector Chen keeps his word,' Yu cut in. 'I've been his partner for years, I know.'

'Now Detective Yu wants me to make this conference call about the yellow mask serial murder—'

'Yellow mask serial murder?'

'The yellow masks come from the Shanghai Number One People's Hospital, in which your wife passed away, I know, and I'm sincerely sorry about it. So many people get terribly sick because of the contaminated air, and the hospital provides the specially treated masks to the in-house patients against cross-infection, and to their visiting family members and the hospital staff members, too.'

There was no immediate response from Lou. Yu thought he detected a nervous twitching at the corner of the man's mouth.

'It's not too far-fetched to see the connection between the illness and the air pollution, I understand. Much more should have been done about the environmental crisis, like the documentary I've mentioned, to call people's attention to the disaster. Of course, there are ways of striving for that purpose. In your case, you planted the yellow masks at the crime scenes – in a symbolic protest against the catastrophic pollution. In memory of her, but also much more than that. As a wake-up call to reach as many people as possible, what could have worked out more effectively than a sensational serial murder?'

Lou still made no response, but he breathed more heavily. Yu pushed a cup of water across the table to him.

'In that way, you're trying to immortalize her memory in a unique way—'

'Don't say any more!'

'But I don't think the government will ever let the message of the yellow mask serial murder be known.'

'I don't know what you're talking about, Chief Inspector Chen, but in the age of *Weixin* and *Weibo*, things may spread around really quickly.'

'With you in custody, Internal Security will do everything imaginable to make sure not a single word of that message of yours ever comes out. On that much you can trust me, Lou.'

'You cannot lock me up for more than two or three days with neither evidence nor witness, can you?'

'For cops like Detective Yu and me, we cannot. But what about Internal Security? They're above the law, and they don't play by any rules. In fact, they are going to charge another man for the serial murder, in a scenario far less politically damaging to the government. In the meantime, they can keep you locked up as long as they like. In the name of the Party's interests, they can easily lock you up in secret.'

'With her gone, what do I have to care about in this world – except for her memory?'

'But I have to say something for the victims—'

'You don't have to give me a lecture about law and justice, Chief Inspector Chen. What about victims like Shen, so many more of them, now and in the future? You think you want to save lives? More will be lost if the environmental crisis goes on like this.'

It was the first time that Lou did not make a downright denial. On the contrary, he seemed to be arguing into the scenario suggested by the inspector.

'Whatever justification you may have in mind, as a cop I cannot let it go on, taking more innocent victims down the road,' Chen said firmly. 'On the other hand, however, I think I can give you a promise – or two.'

'Come on, a promise or two from you? How many times has the Beijing government given out promises about the clean air?'

'I cannot agree more with you, Lou. I'm not promising anything about what the government may or may not do, but about what I will do. Not just as a cop, but as a writer, too. Your late wife might have read some of my works. In fact, I have written a poem about the polluted Tai Lake, called "Don't Cry, Tai Lake" in *Shanghai Literature*.'

'Don't be surprised about anything done by Chief Inspector Chen.' Yu could not help joining in once again, though it seemed so bookish of Chen to start talking about poetry at this moment. 'Yes, my wife Peiqin has also read that poem.'

'To prove it, I'm sending you an electronic link to the poem published in the magazine. You can read it on the phone. Ironically, that's the reason why I've been given the job from the Party Central Discipline Committee – as one familiar with the environmental issues.'

'But what's that to do with your promise, Poet-Inspector Chen?'

'I'm going to write a story about you and your wife set in the background of the environmental disaster. Not with your real names, but your message won't get lost.'

'How could a Party-member chief inspector choose to do that?'

'Can you guess where I'm making the phone call to you? Bund Park. Detective Yu has joked with me about it being a feng shui place for me.'

'I've just said so to him earlier this morning,' Yu said in a hurry, though confounded.

'Years ago, still in the middle of the Cultural Revolution, I studied English there, an experience that eventually led to my career as a cop, a career I had never dreamed about in the park at the time. All these years, whenever I had to make a difficult decision, I would go back to the park. Life is like a long chain of misplaced yin/yang causalities. So what do I have to really worry about if I am not a Party-member chief inspector but a nobody just like in the days of English study here?'

'What are you driving at?' Lou looked up in surprise.

'I'm here at the park this morning because the decision about the environmental project may cost me the Party membership as well as the chief inspectorship. But it's the right decision for me to make, I believe. And the same with the decision to write the story I have just promised.'

'You really mean it, Inspector Chen?'

'It may take time to have a story written, and to get it published. With the censorship in China, there's no guarantee of a publishing date I can give you, I have to be honest about it. But I'll have it done, I promise.'

It was something totally unexpected. The story would not appear to be politically correct, but Chen would have it written as promised, Yu knew for sure.

'Yes, it will make a world of difference to her memory,' Yu said in a hurry. 'If she could have known in the nether world, it would have been a huge comfort for her to know that the message is out there.'

Lou looked confounded for a second or two, shaking his head in confusion before something changed in his expression.

'Then what's the second promise from you?'

'I'll make a seven-seven service in memory of her, and do that in a Buddhist temple. I will send pictures of the service to you afterward.'

'A Buddhist service. You really will do that?'

'My mother is a devoted Buddhist believer. She did that for my late father many years ago, so I know how important it is. I'm not sure if I can book it under your name, but it will be a service dedicated to her name. As a cop, I have no choice, but that's the least—'

'I've heard about you, Chief Inspector Chen. You honestly mean it?'

'Yes, I have to consult my mother about the details, and I swear on her name I will do that.'

'Chief Inspector Chen will do what he believes as the right thing for him to do,' Yu chipped in, though stunned just like Lou about the unbelievable offer from the inspector, 'in spite of all the trouble he may get into.'

'Confucius says, "Knowing it's impossible for you to do the thing, you still have to try as long as it's the right thing for you to do." But it may not be too much trouble to write a story or arrange a Buddhist service. You don't have to exaggerate for me, Detective Yu.'

Lou did not say anything immediately, his head hung low, his face bleached of color.

Inspector Chen waited on the other end of the line, and Yu waited too.

'I'll take a look first at the poem you are sending over,'

Lou finally said, his voice hoarse all of a sudden. 'And then I will say what I want to say to your partner, Detective Yu. Except for her memories, what else should I care about in this world?'

'Let me say this again, Lou. The case aside, the story about your wife and you is soul-touching, and I too will do whatever possible for her memories.' Chen continued after a short pause, raising his voice, 'Send Lou's statement to me afterward, Detective Yu.'

At seven forty-five, Inspector Chen arrived at Bian's factory, which was operating with three shifts to cope with the ever-increasing demand for air products. He saw a group of female night-shift workers walking out the factory gate, their faces wan, haggard against the opaqueness of the morning.

But he felt pretty much energized for the moment. Perhaps the park was really a feng shui place for him, though he was not so sure about the result of what had happened there.

Bian was taken aback at his unannounced visit to his office so early in the morning.

'Oh, it's you, Chief Inspector Chen. What wind has brought you over to my office today? Yes, you saw Yuan Jing – oh, Shanshan – at the meeting in the club the other day, didn't you?'

'Yes. I did. Do you have a few minutes for me, Bian?'

'Sure,' Bian said, closing the office door. 'What did she say to you?'

'She did not see me.'

'What do you mean, Chief Inspector Chen?'

'I was just the one sitting in the audience, making notes but putting in no comments, like an unobtrusive representative of yours, exactly the way I promised you. I don't think she recognized me.'

'So . . .'

But it was not a moment for Chen to explain so many things converging altogether. In fact, he could hardly explain them to himself.

'The documentary has to be released as soon as possible. Way ahead of the original schedule. Don't wait any more,

Bian. It's so urgent. For all of you involved in the making of the documentary, and particularly for Shanshan.'

'But she may not yet be done with it.'

'It's a good documentary as it is. A finishing touch could be nice, but it won't make too much difference. It has to be put online at the earliest date possible. Definitely it has to be earlier—'

'Earlier than what, Chief Inspector Chen?'

'I cannot afford to go into details here, Bian. Suffice it to say, if the documentary is not released in time, all the efforts you have put in could go to waste.'

'I don't know much about its scheduled release date, but I've heard people talking about their preference for a date after the conclusion of the National People's Congress in Beijing. In two or three weeks, I think.'

Chen understood their preference for its release after the ending of the session. Though it was nothing but a routine practice of rubber stamping in the name of the people's power, the government did not want anything to interfere with the grand political show. The Party authorities could be so upset with a documentary about smog-smothered China, an immediate ban would be implemented.

'Under the normal circumstances, I would say it's a workable idea, your original plan about the release date.'

There was no direct response from Bian, who then said, looking straight into Chen's eyes, 'I don't really understand what you're talking about, Chief Inspector Chen. But if the situation is that serious, you may have to talk to Shanshan in person. She's the one in charge.'

'There's a point in your argument.' Only he was in no position to go to Shanshan in person, for personal as well as political reasons. But how could he tell this to Bian?

On the spur of the moment, he pulled out of the large envelope the copy of *Shanghai Literature*.

Opening the magazine to the page with the poem on it, he wrote on the upper right corner, 'To my muse at the dorm room and the Cadre Recreation Center by Tai Lake.' Then he signed his name underneath.

'When you give her the message about the urgency of

posting the documentary online, show her the magazine. Tell her the message is from a man who was inspired by her for the writing of the poem. She will understand, and make the decision accordingly.'

He put the magazine back into the envelope, which bore the letterhead of the Shanghai Police Bureau, he noted. It did not matter, though. She must have long guessed his true identity. It was perhaps the very reason that she had tried not to contact him, even after she set up the office in the city of Shanghai.

Around nine, Inspector Chen walked into an eatery advertising 'four authentic Shanghai morning snacks' – the earthen oven cake, fried dough stick, fried rice cake and bean soup. These used to be cheap yet popular street snacks in the days of his English studies at Bund Park, but in a collective nostalgia of the city, they were staging a comeback.

The eatery was quite a shabby one, where he took the hot earthen oven cake and fried dough stick from the chef standing by the stove. But instead of digging into the snacks while walking away like most customers, he seated himself at a wobbly, greasy table inside.

In fact, it was the one and only table there, with him as the only customer. With the noise of other customers as well as the fumes and heat from the stove and woks, it was not comfortable to sit inside, he knew.

But all of a sudden, he was just inexplicably tired, having done all he could have done.

And he thought of a young woman biting into the earthen oven cake, licking the sesame from her lips on her way back to the office in the early morning, just a few days ago.

Then his cellphone buzzed.

It was an email with attachment from Detective Yu.

Lou confessed readily after the phone conference in the backroom of the neighborhood committee office.

In fact, Lou had prepared a detailed statement in his cellphone to be released online upon the completion of the seven-seven ritual, with the seventh victim claimed, or at the moment of his being surrounded by the police. It was because the preemptive strike caught him off guard, so he did not have the time to do anything about it.

I'm attaching his pre-prepared statement here, and I shall follow up with more information.

Chen downloaded the statement and began reading.

The statement was quite a long one, which began with an account of the love-at-first-sight romance between Lou, an IT technician in his mid-twenties, and Shen, a sales manager at a computer store, two years younger. Falling for each other, the two soon became inseparable. There was only one hurdle to their much-dreamed-about future. In the city of Shanghai, it was of absolute necessity for a young man to have an apartment under his own name. It was a convention developed out of an increasingly materialistic society, but it was also seen as a realistic insistence on the part of her parents. Under Mao, it had been quite common for a family of two or even three generations to stay squeezed in one room, but with the changes of the economic reform launched by Deng, it was now considered the norm for a young couple to live out of their own space. Shen's parents vetoed the idea of Lou's parents measuring out a partitioned cubicle for the young couple, as well as their plan of renting an apartment first. It was not easy for young people to save up enough money with the housing prices continuously soaring up. The price for one square meter at seventy thousand yuan actually equaled a whole year's income for Lou. So the two young people had to put off their wedding plans, one year after another, working overtime or at several jobs to save enough for the down payment. After five or six years, her parents finally relented, letting them settle on an old one-bedroom apartment in Zabei instead of a new two-bedroom property in Xuhui. It took all their savings, but they moved in and got married.

Still on the honeymoon, she started to have a persistent cough. Possibly because of the new paint in the old apartment, or because of her working too hard for the last several years. He bought her some herbs as well as antibiotics. But with her cough not going away, he took her to see a doctor who diagnosed her as suffering from lung cancer – at the fourth stage. How was it possible? She did not smoke. Nor did he. The doctor showed them a chart showing a large number of people suffering from lung cancer because of the polluted air. In the hospital she fought a hard battle, holding his hand, trying all the treatments available, but to no avail. In less than four months, she passed away one early smoggy morning.

He was devastated. For days after her death, he continued going to the hospital like one possessed, clinging to the momentary illusion, as if she were still there, waiting for him.

His family became so worried. With the end of the first week after her death drawing near, they suggested that he observe the seven-seven ritual with a special meal dedicated to her. Preparing her favorite dishes would keep him too busy, they hoped, to dwell on her memories. He went to the market, shopping like crazy, but on the seventh morning, he went out to the hospital like before.

To him, the walk to the hospital in the morning was a ritual far more meaningful. But that morning, he happened to see the night caregiver surnamed Peng leaving the hospital. She was wearing a yellowish mask, but he recognized her.

About two weeks before Shen's death, he had had an argument with Peng, who had stopped taking care of Shen properly because of his failure to pay the fee in time. With the soaring medical expenses, he was running out of money. Peng was not to blame. She had to take care of five or six patients at night. It made sense for her to be more attentive to those paying her promptly. But it was so painful to see Shen writhing in pain, unattended, he recalled.

At that moment, all of a sudden, the scene of Peng leaving the hospital pushed him over the edge. He started following her in the direction of the Bund. Initially, it was no more than an impulsive reaction, but with Peng moving closer to the bridge, he was seized with an unbreathable panic about her disappearing into the crowds. He hastened to pick up a heavy brick from a construction site, rushed up, and knocked at her head from behind. One single blow and she fell without any struggle. Bending over to pull the yellowish mask off her face, he found her already unconscious.

It was at that moment that he was galvanized with a sense of doing something really meaningful in Shen's memory. Much more than a special meal in observation of the seven-seven ritual.

At that moment, he also knew in a flash what he was going to do for the following six weeks. Something like a list of things and people responsible for Shen's early death came up in a ghastly smog in his mind. The catastrophic air pollution at the top, because of the governmental GDP-oriented policy; the skyrocketing housing prices, for which she had worked so hard for years; the Party propaganda about the clean air and the blue sky; the terrible attitude from the caregiver at the hospital . . .

All of a sudden, he felt he could breathe freely for the first time since Shen's death, gazing at the yellowish mask on the ground.

It was quite a providence that he too had several yellowish masks gathered at home. He calculated in his mind – enough for his purpose.

And it would serve as an unmistakable sign, symbolizing the cause and effect of their tragedy, and calling for people's attention to the national disaster.

As for what would happen to him, he hardly cared. Everything was finished for him with her death, and he was nothing but a 'walking corpse' – except for the delivery of his ultimate statement at the ending of the seven-seven. That was the only good thing he believed he could do for her. And in a frenzied figment of his imagination, for the whole society, too. Things could not go on like this. It would be the ultimate wake-up call about the disastrous consequences, to which everyone had to pay serious attention: 'With air quality like this, many more people, and even those much younger, would turn into victims.'

The statement also gave a quite detailed account of the serial murder from the very beginning – from the chance encounter with the first victim Peng, to the premeditated killing of the subsequent victims.

The location of the first victim near the Bund Bridge and the Bund prompted him to look for other central locations for a large audience.

As for the attack time, Lou did not have to think too much about it. Shen had breathed her last breath in the early morning, before six.

For the second victim, Lou targeted the weather bureau, which had been forecasting the clear, clean air for years as the governmental mouthpiece. It proved to be too difficult to ambush the head of the bureau, who did not appear so early in the morning. So Lou thought that an anchorman would be symbolic enough, but he was unable to take action on the second seventh day, not just because of those surveillance cameras installed all over the People's Square, but also because no one walked out of the bureau so early that morning. So he attacked on the eighth day instead, as Linghu walked out of the weather bureau wearing a mask. It saved Lou a mask.

As for the third victim, Yan, Lou chose her for a different reason. She was a salesperson for one of the new apartments Lou had looked at in Lujiazui, but when he came up with the amount available for the down payment, she practically drove him out. The price had shot up like crazy in a couple of days. The uncontrollable housing prices were not a problem she had created, but her refusal to be flexible was something he could not forget. He knew about Yan's jogging in the morning, and Lujiazui made the perfect location for the crime. With eight days passed between the first and second victims, he waited for only six days for Yan. He tried to follow the time pattern of the ritual killing.

As for the fourth victim, Xiang, Lou had no idea about the video in the background. Nor about her husband being Geng. Lou was just so angry with the official media for its silence about the air pollution. He had once worked on a network program for a kindergarten school close to the *Wenhui* building, so knew there were people working at the newspaper for the night. She fell prey on her way back to the *Wenhui* office, still having the earthen oven cake in her hand. It happened to be a windy morning. As he planted the mask beside her, he put the half-eaten cake on top, lest it would be blown away.

As for the one in the New World, he had simply run out of symbolic targets. Another murder in a central location would have called for a lot of attention, particularly with the speculation about the serial murders already abuzz online.

He did have a specific one in mind for the seventh-seven, though: the former government spokesperson who had repudiated the air quality report of the American Embassy. For some reason, the spokesperson now worked as an official in the Shanghai Propaganda Ministry.

Lou was not unaware of lives being lost for his plan; to him, they were just the unavoidable casualties for a must-fight battle.

After reading through the statement, Inspector Chen was not in a hurry to leave the eatery. In addition, he had a bowl of steaming hot soybean soup with dried shrimp and purple seaweed after an old waiter had walked to the table a couple of times.

He was sad, placing the cellphone beside the bowl without taking a spoonful of it.

The earthen oven cake was already cold, and the fried dough stick limpid; he had neither the mood nor the appetite to finish the Shanghai snack.

It was also long after the breakfast hour.

Picking up his cellphone, he pulled out the draft of his report saved on the phone and started writing a postscript for Zhao.

P.S. Remember the case I told you about, Comrade Secretary Zhao, when I first got the assignment from you at the Hyatt Hotel? I've been concentrating on your assignment, but as you may imagine, Party Secretary Li and other colleagues in the bureau have kept me in the loop about the progress of the investigation.

Just this morning, my partner, Detective Yu, has informed me that the criminal in the 'yellow mask serial murder' was caught in the New World, another central location of the city. You don't have the time for the details of the investigation, I understand. In a nutshell, it is a serial murder committed by a grief-distraught husband surnamed Lou, whose wife Shen recently died of lung cancer, possibly a victim of the air pollution. Lou set out to avenge her by killing persons he saw as related to her death. And he planted the masks beside the bodies as his signature; also as a protest against the air pollution that claimed her life.

It might not necessarily have been true, with so many possible causes for the disease, but she was young and she never smoked. Lou insisted on seeing the cause and effect here, and he struck out in a frenzied plan – one victim on a seven-day cycle, in observance of the seven-seven ritual service to her memory. The serial murder, if not stopped, would have continued and coincided with the session of the National People's Congress. That could of course have been so disastrous in its political impact.

With the justification resonant in his twisted mind, he prepared a message to be released upon the completion of the seven-seven ceremony. The statement ends like this:

'Personally, there's nothing left for me in the world with her departure from it. After the seven-seven, everything will be finished for me. So I want to send a message. It's a matter of time for many more people, millions and millions of people, to fall prey to the disastrous pollution. So it's a call to arms. Maybe it's not too late. If so, I have done something meaningful for her.'

There's no excusing the killings, but what he says about 'a matter of time' worries me. I shudder at the consequences if we don't do anything about it. This time, it's just by a stroke of luck that Detective Yu caught him. But luck cannot always be on our side.

There's no telling whether there could be another case like this, or when. Such crimes have to be stopped, but I could not help putting myself in his shoes. His blaming the uncontrollable air pollution for his wife's death is not without some justification.

In spite of the tremendous progress China has made in its unprecedented reform, the social stability would be shattered if people were unable to have clean air for long.

So we have to convince our people that our Party government is doing everything possible on their side. For that purpose, the documentary I've told you about might really help.

And this time, he clicked the send button.

EPILOGUE

The next day, Party Secretary Li had a busy day in the Shanghai Police Bureau.

In a press conference arranged at a moment's notice, Li took over the job of talking to the media, declaring that the 'yellow mask serial murder case' had been solved, though he didn't bring up any details.

'Let me say this first, it's because of the excellent work done by Chief Inspector Chen together with his long-time partner Detective Yu that the case has been successfully solved.'

It looked just like another shrewd move on the part of Li, Detective Yu observed, without making a comment there.

Li had to give credit where it was due, particularly with Chen seen as being in Zhao's favor. It might also have been a lesson Li had just learned. For crucial cases like this, at a crucial moment, he still needed Chen, so he had to openly sing the praises of the chief inspector. And last but not least, Li did not have to answer any questions too difficult for him.

'For the serial murder case, the perpetrator was pushed over the edge at the death of his wife, killing at random. As for the detailed information, you'll have to talk to Chief Inspector Chen. We have discussed it numerous times, but he really excels in criminology. In the meantime, he has been engaged with another important job from Beijing, therefore is too busy to come to the press conference today. He'll go over the case with you as soon as possible, and as much as possible too. In short, under the leadership of our great Party, the Shanghai Police Bureau is confident of keeping the city secure and safe for the people.'

Li was indeed a seasoned talker, always politically correct. Yu produced a cigarette, shaking his head.

* * *

Inspector Chen had been engaged with another investigation, though not the one Party Secretary Li had mentioned in the press conference, from Comrade Secretary Zhao.

Chen had just learned from Melong some clues to the identity of the secret video holder: Miao Dehua, the son of a former rival ruthlessly crushed by Geng in the Party system. Miao had purchased the video for a staggering amount of money, for revenge, waiting for the most damaging moment to release it online. With the unexpected death of Xiang, holding it any longer could be less damaging for Geng, so Miao lost no time posting it on the Internet.

With the serial murder case solved, and with so many exposures of corruption in the Party system, people no longer paid attention to the video scandal like before. It was hinted in the official media that one of the anti-government netizens had posted the video online, and that it was a matter of time before such a law-breaking netizen would be punished, but for the moment, that was about it.

It was not a case under his investigation anyway, Chief Inspector Chen concluded.

Two days later, Chen got a short text message from Zhao.

'Congratulations! Another marvelous job you have done, Comrade Chief Inspector Chen. I know I can count on you.'

It was vague, and Chen knew better than to push for clarification, but he could sense a touch of sincerity, he thought, on the part of the senior Party leader.

It did not mean that Zhao agreed with the points made in his report, particularly those about the air pollution and the documentary. It would be too much of a responsibility for anyone to be specific, but it was a responsibility Inspector Chen was more than willing to take.

Two days later, the documentary 'Hold Your Breath, China' was released online, ahead of its original schedule.

With its simultaneous appearance on the major websites all over the country, it was said to have been viewed about thirty million times in China within the first two days of its release.

The discussions about China's air pollution as explored and

researched in the documentary immediately overwhelmed other news, including the 'yellowish mask serial murder case' in Shanghai, much to the relief of Party Secretary Li and his people.

For some unknown reason, the Beijing government did not hasten, for once, to make a visible effort to block the documentary, in spite of the frenzied discussion among the netizens.

Even more unbelievably, there came some positive mentions of the documentary in the official media. The *Guangming Daily* carried a short review commemorating the movie, and quoting a comment by the head of the Public Health Ministry that the documentary did something the people in the ministry had been unable to do for years. It concluded, not too surprisingly, that the CCP stands firmly by the side of the Chinese people in the arduous battle against the environmental crisis.

The review soon found its way into the cyber world, echoing and rippling. A considerable number of netizens took it as a possible sign for some significant change in China's environmental policy.

Three days after the release of the documentary, Beijing witnessed the grand opening of the Thirteenth Session of China's National People's Congress.

During the opening session, one of its agendas was the removal of Kang from his position as a corrupt official responsible for the environmental disaster. In an editorial of the *People's Daily*, Kang's GDP-oriented argument in the interview with Yuan Jing was quoted and repudiated.

The disgraceful fall of Kang was seen as a signal pointing to Yong, the once powerful patron for the gang at the top of the Party system. Yong's absence at the conference was commonly interpreted in connection to it.

However, the heated discussion over the documentary still went on, almost to the extent of drowning out all the political propaganda about the conference in Beijing.

On the third day of the conference, the Party authorities ordered that the documentary be removed from all the websites, and all the comments posted about it deleted or blocked as well.

For once, the official media kept mum about the governmental decision, without so much as trying to hail the abrupt turn as the correct decision by the Party government, or to interpret the meaning of it, as if nothing had happened at all.

But something had already happened in the way of people's thinking.

That same day, Chief Inspector Chen got a notice for him to leave the Shanghai Police Bureau for a Party school seminar in Suzhou.

It was an arrangement of dubious nature. Quite possibly a preliminary step to remove him from his bureau position. Some people in the Forbidden City were not pleased with his recent work, which he understood. But he did not find himself too worried about it.

For the first time in his career, Chen was seriously debating with himself whether he should go on serving as a Party-member chief inspector.

But he would have to do one more thing he'd promised as a chief inspector.

Chief Inspector Chen found himself to be the first one to step into a small Buddhist service hall, possibly the smallest in Longhua Temple.

Even for such a hall, its fee was more than ten thousand yuan, not including that for the script-chant service performed by the monks, the amount of which would have to be calculated by the length of the job. It was quite an expense for Chen, but he thought he could eke it out by quitting smoking and eating out for a month or two.

In spite of his mother's devotion, Chen was not that into Buddhism. As it seemed to him, such services could function at the most as a sort of cold comfort – psychologically, if at all – for the survivors.

But for once, he thought he had no choice.

The head of the monks hurried over, a young man named Yuanjue, who wore a pair of gold-rimmed glasses and handed him a business card with his name and temple position printed in gold: The Number One Abbot Assistant.

'The business is so hot here. But for you, the service would have required booking at least two or three months beforehand. Our abbot has taken your request into special consideration.'

'I appreciate it very much.'

'For you, Chief Inspector Chen, we will also chant for an extra half an hour for free.'

What could that mean? Chen failed to make an instant response.

'Just give people here some red envelopes, Chief Inspector Chen. Don't worry about it.'

But Chen became worried. He did not think he had enough left in his wallet for the red envelopes after paying for the scripture-chanting service.

Then Detective Yu and Peiqin arrived, carrying a variety of conventional offerings for such a Buddhist service.

'Since we are doing it, we have to do it properly,' Peiqin said, arranging on the service table the specially red-sealed cakes, buns, nuts and candies, all of which were supposedly for the benefit of the deceased in the other world.

'She went to Shendacheng Restaurant for these special offerings early in the morning. There's a growing demand for them,' Yu said, raising the camera for pictures.

'Yes, take some pictures,' Chen said, with a touch of sentimentality in spite of himself. 'I'll have them delivered to Lou.'

'Yes, we all understand,' Peiqin said in an abated voice. 'It's a very special seven-seven ceremony. We all have to come.'

'Alas, that's about all we can do.'

Behind the offerings on the table, there was a red-paper-covered tablet that showed a picture of Shen with a radiant smile playing on her lips. None of them in the hall had met her in life. Yu had obtained the picture from the police file. It had been taken in Wangkai, a well-known studio on Nanjing Road, as part of the honeymoon package for the happy newlyweds.

Peiqin perched herself on a stool by the service table and

started folding a bunch of fake money into the shape of ancient silver ingots, for use in the nether world.

To Chen's surprise, Bian and Gu also walked into the service hall in large strides.

How much the two uninvited visitors could have known about the deceased with her name inscribed on the service hall tablet, Chen had no idea.

Bian had called for a celebration banquet for the successful release of the documentary, but Chen could not have made it because of the service at the temple.

'It's for Shen – one of the victims of the air pollution.'

'You mean . . . very well. It's something worth doing, Chief Inspector Chen,' Bian had said, with a surprising resolution in his voice. 'I'll see what I can do.'

Bian must then have told Gu about it, and they came together.

But Chen was glad to see two more people at the service hall. It should not turn out to be a lonely service for her.

The two newcomers stood side by side, holding bunches of tall incense in their hands after bowing respectfully to the tablet.

'You should have told me earlier, Chief Inspector Chen,' Mr Gu said with a complaining note in his voice.

Like always, Gu lost no time entering into the role of a magnanimous businessman. He immediately started distributing a bunch of red envelopes to the monks filed up there, as though having prepared them long beforehand.

'Haven't you heard the old proverb? It won't be so good for "old monks to chant the scripture without putting their hearts and souls into it". Red envelopes are always much appreciated and needed, which makes a world of difference. You cannot help it in today's materialistic society.'

Bian must have learned something else about the deceased. He carried in his hand a large cardboard box. To the surprise of the people there, he took out a fresh air machine made of cardboard, vividly painted and decorated, probably the same size as the real one.

'It's symbolic, I have to say, just pathetically symbolic,' Bian said, shaking his head.

'Oh, I almost forgot,' Gu said. 'Lianping also wants to come here today, but she suffers morning sickness with her pregnancy. So she asks me to take some pictures for her. They may be used for an article.'

In the silence that ensued, the monks started chanting with a flourish of their odd-shaped instruments. People seemed relieved at the realization that they did not have to talk for the moment.

Chen cast another look at the picture on the tablet. It might be as well for her not to know anything – though the inspector did not think she knew – about what had happened since she left the mundane world.

> *Oh, this feeling, to be collected later*
> *in memories, is already confused.*

'Our most honorable patron, you have done something so extraordinary for the deceased today. Don't be so sad any more,' the head monk Yuanjue stepped over and said to him, still counting the beads in his hand. 'You appear to be drenched in sweat, Chief Inspector Chen.'

With the monks' chanting finally reaching a climax, they were moving out for the final part of the service – to burn the nether world money in the courtyard of the temple.

It was there that Bian pulled at Chen's hand and inserted into it a white envelope. The envelope bore a handwriting unrecognizable to him.

With people's attention fixed on the dancing fire of the gold and silver ingots in the bronze burner, Chen retreated into a corner in the courtyard and took the letter out.

The letter presented nothing but a stanza from a poem quoted in Shanshan's last letter to him in Wuxi, along with the last paragraph from that letter.

> *A cloud in the sky, inadvertent, I cast*
> *a shadow in the waves of your heart.*
> *Don't be so amazed,*
> *nor be so dazed –*
> *Just for an instant it may last.*

We meet on the night-covered sea;
You have your destination, and I, mine,
If you remember, that's fine,
But better forget the shine
Enkindled between you and me.

Because of the light produced in our meeting,
however transitory, over the night-covered lake, can
you forgive me for this upset and stay friends?

So she had known all along.

Perhaps as early as that afternoon at the Oriental Club in
the New World, and that's why she had brought up his favorite
Confucian maxim.

With the letter still in his hand, another text message came in
to Chen, with a ding reminiscent of the knock made with the
head monk's fish-shaped wooden instrument. It was from
Ouyang, the editor of *Shanghai Literature.*

'Qiang's body was discovered this morning. Killed by a
violent blow to the back of his head.'

Pocketing the letter in a hurry, Inspector Chen checked Zhao's
schedule sent to him the previous day. The senior Party leader
was leaving Shanghai the next day. Chen would try to arrange
a last-minute meeting with him.

He had to meet with Zhao in person, to talk him into letting
the inspector take care of the investigation into Qiang's death
in Shanghai, instead of going to the Party school seminar in
Suzhou.

They did not have to talk about the documentary or
Shanshan's activities. Sometimes some things were better left
unsaid. Zhao had sent him a short text message of thanks
along with his itinerary. That was about all of it.

But because of it, Zhao might grant his request to investigate the death of Qiang, which could be interpreted as a result
of the inspector's doing the job for Zhao.

Earlier, Chen had hinted about the possibility of his being
shadowed in the midst of his carrying out the investigation. It

would not be too far-fetched to portray Qiang as a collateral casualty. At least it appeared as a convincing scenario to himself.

With the power struggle going on at the top, it might appear convincing to Zhao, too.

The inspector had no idea what he could do for Qiang, but he would try in whatever way possible.

'Knowing it's impossible for you to do the thing, you still have to try as long as it's the right thing for you to do.' He had quoted the Confucian maxim recently, though he failed to recall when.

'What's up?' Yu said, moving over.

Chen knew he must have looked terrible, with the cellphone grasped tight in his trembling hand.

Others were also coming over to Chen, looking at him with concern in their eyes. After all, the enigmatic inspector might not have told them everything.

'The service is finished here,' Peiqin said tentatively.

The fire out in the burner, the gold and silver ingots in ashes, the monks were filing back to the hall.

'I've got to leave now,' Chen said, 'for another case, possibly related.'

CPSIA information can be obtained
at www.ICGtesting.com
Printed in the USA
LVHW041932140820
663225LV00002B/4/J